# KODIAK SECTOR

V-CLAN SERIES

USA TODAY BESTSELLING AUTHOR
# LEXI C. FOSS

This is a work of fiction. Names, characters, places, and incidents are either the product of the author's imagination or are used fictitiously, and any resemblance to actual persons, living or dead, business establishments, events, or locales is entirely coincidental.

*Kodiak Sector*

Editing by Outthink Editing, LLC

Proofreading by: Katie Schmahl & Jean Bachen

Cover Design: Jay R. Villalobos with Covers by Juan

Cover Photography: Michelle Lancaster

Cover Models: David & Darcie

Chapter Page Illustrations: Labyrinth Book Designs

Published by: Ninja Newt Publishing, LLC

Digital Edition

ISBN: 978-1-68530-365-5

Print Edition

ISBN: 978-1-68530-412-6

**AI Disclaimer: This book does not contain any elements of AI content. All art was designed by real artists, and all of the words were written by the author.**

*To my fated mate, thank you for being my partner in life and an amazing father to our son.*

# KODIAK SECTOR

V-CLAN SERIES

# KODIAK SECTOR

Welcome to Kodiak Sector, home to the most vicious
Alphas in the Z-Clan world.
It's a deadly place for an Omega like me.
But my intended mate is determined to drag me back to
the hell I came from, all to save his sister.

He thinks I know how to find her.
I don't.
I just *see* things. Like the future.
And right now, it's full of savagery and pain.

Until suddenly, my visions disappear.
Suggesting a fate worse than death.
One I begin to understand when I go into heat in the
Nomad Lands near Kodiak Sector.

My intended mate is suddenly forced to choose—me or his
sister?
For once, I can't see what will happen.
But in my heart, I know who he'll save.
*Because no one ever picks me.*

**Author's Note:** *Kodiak Sector* is a fast-paced standalone
shifter romance featuring a dark world with knotting,
nesting, growling, and a whole hell of a lot of purring.

# A NOTE FROM LEXI

*Kodiak Sector* is a standalone romance story in the V-Clan/Z-Clan universe. No other books need to be read prior to this one to follow the storyline. That said, Ashlyn and Grey first met in *Eclipse Sector*. So, if you prefer a chronological experience, I would go back to read *Eclipse Sector* first.

This is a fast-paced shifter romance with strong Omegaverse themes. There are Alpha/Omega dynamics, nesting, purring, estrous cycles, and, of course, *knotting*. If you're unfamiliar with these terms, don't worry—they're explained throughout the book.

Those of you familiar with Omegaverse themes may want to know if this is dark or sweet—it's a dark world with a sweeter romance. I honestly expected a lot more angst (given Ashlyn's voice in my head), but Grey's straightforward nature made him much easier to wrangle than stubborn Cillian.

On that note, if you prefer angst and longer books, I recommend *Eclipse Sector*.

If you like shorter, fast-burn romances, then I hope you enjoy Grey and Ashlyn's story.

Final note, there is an overarching story arc that will continue into *Lunar Sector* and potentially the Drakon-Clan series. However, the romance is a complete standalone with a happily-ever-after ending.

## Kodiak Sector Content Highlights:

✓ Consent Between Hero & Heroine

  ✓ Quick Read/Fast-Burn

  ✓ Dark Content Involving Mentions of Nonconsent Behavior Between Other Alphas and Omegas (not the hero with his heroine)

  ✓ Heroine Fears a Potential Future Assault (Spoiler for those concerned: There are mentions of this throughout and a scene that borders on experiencing this from her point of view — **There is no actual assault in this book.**)

  ✓ Low Angst

  ✓ No Other Woman or Other Man Drama (No Cheating)

  ✓ Pregnancy

  ✓ Primal Energy

  ✓ Possessive Over the Top Alpha Male

  ✓ Touch Her and Die Vibes

  ✓ Knotting, Nesting, Purring, Growling (I mean, obviously the book wouldn't be complete without these things, right?)

Enjoy! <3

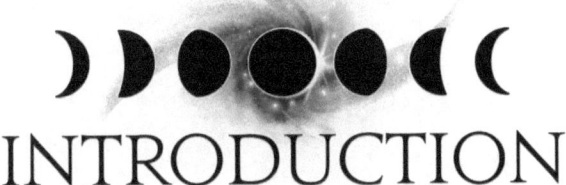

# INTRODUCTION

Nearly a century ago, a zombielike virus spread across the globe, destroying over ninety percent of the human race. Many of the supernatural species of the world were immune to the plague. Others were not.

Those who have survived—both human and supernatural alike—now rule their own territories, otherwise known as sectors.

You're about to enter the V-Clan world, a breed of shifter wolves with vampiric traits. These beings prefer the night. They thrive on magic. And perhaps most importantly of all, the Alphas of this kind cherish their Omega mates.

*Kodiak Sector* is a unique hybrid novel that also ventures into the Z-Clan world, which is a kingdom full of feral Alphas that shift into wolves the size of polar bears. They're intense. They're mean. And they are *not* kind to their Omegas.

This is a dark future. Some of the supernatural species are far more violent than others in existence. That will become apparent in this novel.

# PROLOGUE

## GREY

### Kodiak Sector

Ice floods my veins as I take in the sight before me.

The sensation has nothing to do with the frigid surroundings, the frosty air, or the wintry conditions of Kodiak Sector. And everything to do with the frozen Omega lying in the water.

*Fuck.*

It took me far too long to decode this female's cryptic notes in her damn journals.

I want to throttle her for not being more forthcoming.

And drop to my knees in apology for allowing this fate to befall her.

I'm about to do the latter when I catch the shiver of her bottom lip, the bluish tint resembling death. Her shoulders tremble next, the shudder undeniable as she gasps a little, like she's just stirred from a nap.

But then her teeth begin to chatter, and I suddenly become aware that I'm just wasting precious fucking time.

Because she's very much alive and in pain.

*From taking a literal ice bath to mask her sweet scent*, I think, sighing inside. A foolish yet intelligent choice.

Shaking my head, I step forward, ready to begin whatever game we're about to play with one another.

"All right, little riddler," I say, letting her know that I'm here and that she can knock off this charade.

But as her eyes flutter open, I realize this isn't an act at all.

She is literally dying in this ice water.

*Dying* whilst waiting for me.

I'm back to wanting to throttle her again.

Only, she's looking at me like I'm the warmth she's been waiting for, the sun she craves, the heat she desperately needs.

Yet that hero-worshipping look morphs into a glimmer of fear, one that threatens to make my heart beat a little faster. "Y-you're here," she stammers out, her voice barely audible.

My brow furrows, and I hold out my hand, confused by her shifting emotions. "Let's get you somewhere warm," I offer.

She considers me for a moment, almost as though she's debating whether or not to trust me.

I suppose I am covered in blood from the battle in Blood Sector, but I came straight here after finally understanding Ashlyn's cryptic note. There hadn't been time for a shower.

I'm about to apologize, debating if that's what the Omega needs to hear before she'll accept my hand, when howls erupt in the distance.

*Never mind*, I think, leaning down and snatching the female from the freezing water. *Fuck, how long has she been lying here?* I wonder, noting the icy sensations trickling up my arms in response to her chilled skin.

2

Rather than voice any of that aloud, I shadow us to a safer location. Somewhere *warmer*.

Not too far away, though, as we have unfinished business in Kodiak Sector. But far enough away to ensure her protection while she recovers from her ice bath.

We materialize in a cave that I've fashioned into one of my many lairs.

Recognition kisses Ashlyn's features, telling me she's foreseen this. Just as I'm sure she's foreseen a great many things.

Which makes her choice of locations in Kodiak Sector somewhat of a mystery to me.

*Why did you allow yourself to nearly freeze to death?* I want to demand.

But, instead, I grab a blanket from a nearby couch and wrap it around her naked body—a body I would have admired a lot more if it weren't fucking blue.

That doesn't stop me from holding her close, though.

She's shivering so hard it's a miracle she hasn't bitten her own tongue.

I pinch her chin and tilt her head back so I can stare into her big blue eyes. She looks so small in my arms, so *fragile*.

And I fucking hate that.

Omegas are meant to be cherished, not abused.

Yet I feel responsible for her current pain. Which is ridiculous since I'm not the one who put her in that water. She did that to herself.

But I am the one who took forever to decode her cryptic notes.

Notes I didn't even realize were for me until several minutes ago.

Ashlyn and I... we don't actually know each other. We've met, yes. But she doesn't really know me. And other than her being a Z-Clan Omega who clearly recognized me the first time we met—suggesting she's had visions of me in the past—I don't truly know her.

Not beyond what I've read in her journals, anyway.

Journals that I only had access to because she left them to be found. She wanted them to be read, too. That's why she dropped all those clues on how to find her in Kodiak Sector.

Only, that's not all she wrote about...

"I'm going to warm you up," I promise her, my gaze still searching hers. "Then we're going to talk about those little notes in your journal about Nikiski. And afterward, you're going to help me find her."

Because Nikiski owns my heart.

I've been hunting for her for years.

My sweet Omega.

My charge.

*My little sister...*

# ASHLYN

## Nomad Lands, Alaska

*Come on, Ash,* I tell myself. *Just… just go out there and face fate.*

I'm not this meek Omega. I'm a powerful seer. I… I don't *hide* in bathrooms.

Except, the Alpha of my literal dreams is standing just outside the door.

My future mate.

My *intended*.

I only know that because of my oracle-like gifts, which are both a blessing and a curse. A blessing because I can use them to help others. A curse because they never actually help me.

*Ugh.* Sometimes seeing the future really shoots stars.

Grabbing the marble counter, I close my eyes and fight the urge to growl.

I've been hiding in here since Grey deposited me in the bath an hour ago. But I can't stop thinking about his strong arms, how they wrapped around me in protective bands as he shadowed me to one of his lairs.

7

*Fates, I can't believe this is finally happening...*

I waited for Grey on the icy shores of Kodiak Sector for days. I almost worried he wouldn't arrive.

But then he did.

And now we're here.

*With me hiding in his bathroom like a coward.*

I wince.

*Enough.*

I am not this woman.

I'm a Z-Clan Omega who has survived hell.

I can survive this destiny, too.

Straightening my spine, I head toward the door, aware that all I'm wearing is a robe. But Grey didn't give me any clothes. Probably because he doesn't have any that will fit me.

I'm only five foot three.

Grey is... well, he's at least a foot taller than me. Probably closer to six foot four. His Z-Clan genetics make him rather large.

*I bet his wolf is huge, too.*

And other parts of him.

I clear my throat. *Don't think about the Alpha's knot, Ash. Or his beast. Just... just step through the threshold and—*

A knock sounds at the door, making me jump backward with a yelp.

"Ashlyn?" Grey's deep tones easily carry through the wood. "Are you all right?"

"Um." I close my eyes and take a breath.

*This is ridiculous. Stop hiding and go face your fate,* I tell myself.

Sighing, I return to the door and gingerly push it open.

"I'm... I'm fine," I tell him. "Just... just adjusting to the temperature change." *What a ridiculous statement.* I'm a shifter. I was healed and fine within five minutes of arriving here. He knows that. I know that. But, fortunately, he doesn't call me on it.

Instead, all he does is nod, like he understands, and takes a step back. "I made you some food."

I blink at him, feeling even more like a lost fool. "Oh." These are the types of things I typically foresee, but with Grey, my sight is... abnormal. "Thank you?"

He frowns at me, probably because my gratitude sounded like a question.

Because, well, I don't know. "I'm sorry," I say, shaking my head. "This is all just..." I pinch my lips to the side. "Can we start over?"

He arches a light-colored brow. "Start over?"

"Like... meet again?" I ask.

He leans against the wall, his thick arms folding and drawing my gaze down to his tight white shirt. It's clean. Crisp. *Smells like fresh snowfall on evergreens.*

I frown. "I didn't realize this lair had more than one shower." In all my visions of this place, I only ever saw a single bedroom with an attached en-suite bathroom, as well as a small living area with a kitchenette and table.

*Maybe this isn't the lair from my visions?* I think, glancing around again, frowning. *No. No, this is definitely where it all happens...*

Grey observes me with his glacial stare. "It doesn't."

"Oh." There's that word again. *Super eloquent, Ash,* I mutter to myself. *You're doing great.*

"I took a dip outside," Grey says, still scrutinizing me with his icy gaze. "It was cold, but it got the job done." He runs his fingers through his damp blond hair, the edges of which reach his massive shoulders. "And no, little riddler. We can't *meet again*." He pushes away from the wall. "Because we've never actually *met*."

I gape at his back as he heads toward the small table with two chairs. He pulls one out, then glances back at me.

"My name is Grey," he murmurs. "I'm half V-Clan Alpha, half Z-Clan Alpha. I'm one of Prince Cael's Elites from Lunar Sector. But, of course, you already know all that. It was on my Alpha candidate card for the mating program."

He leaves the chair for me and takes the opposite one, his movements reminding me of a stealth panther more than a beastly polar bear.

Which is interesting because Z-Clan Alphas tend to be very large in wolf form—very bearlike. Not catlike.

"Hmm," I hum, more to myself than to him, because I'm intrigued. I like this Alpha.

Of course, I've dreamt of him my whole life, our fates always destined to intertwine.

So I'm slightly biased in his favor.

Still, I appreciate him humoring me.

"I'm Ashlyn, Z-Clan Omega," I tell him softly as I join him at the table. "I didn't join the mating program to find a mate, but I suspect you already know that, too."

"I do," he murmurs. "Z-Clan wolves rely on fate." It's not a question, but a statement.

However, I still feel the need to reply, "Yes."

He doesn't immediately comment, instead picking up my bowl and spooning something into it from the pot between us.

*Spaghetti*, I realize, somewhat amused by his choice.

"You joined the mating pool because you knew something was going to happen to the other Omegas," he says, again as a statement, not a question. "And to meet me."

"Yes," I admit. "But also no."

That eyebrow of his lifts again, the color the same as his blond hair.

"I participated because I wanted to help the Omegas," I clarify. "But I didn't realize you would be there." That's why I fell into an icy lake the first time he appeared. That's not how I predicted we would meet for the first time.

Not that we actually did meet... which he just pointed out.

We barely said anything to each other at all.

He simply jumped into the water and pulled me out of it, then Alpha Cillian escorted me back to the igloos in Glacier Sector.

*Maybe that's our thing*, I think. *Meeting in ice water.*

"Lying is a trait I strongly dislike, Omega," Grey informs me flatly.

"I'm not lying, Alpha," I promise him.

His expression darkens, the air between us seeming to chill. "Queen Quinnlynn informed you of my intent to participate. You approved it."

"Well, yes, I did. However, the moment we first saw each other wasn't the moment I saw in my visions," I advise him. "You stated that I joined the mating program to meet you. I corrected your assumption—I joined prior to learning you were participating. I did not anticipate meeting you during the program."

His brow furrows. "Then when were we to meet?"

"In..." I close my eyes and sigh. "Off the shores of Kodiak Sector. That's where my visions of you begin."

He says nothing.

Then I hear him twirling noodles in his bowl with small, meticulous motions.

I peek at him through my lashes and find him still staring at me, but not with that dark expression anymore.

He just looks interested now. "What else have you foreseen between us, Seer?"

"You want to know about your sister," I translate.

"I want to know everything," he corrects me. "And I would also like you to eat. Please."

I look down at my bowl, my lips twisting a little.

"Don't like spaghetti?" he asks.

"No, I do, it's just…" I look at him. "The red sauce makes me think of the blood you were wearing when you picked me up from the water." My nose crinkles. "I assume Prince Tadhg is dead?"

Prince Tadhg is the monster who shadowed me to Kodiak Sector and left me to be violated and killed by all of the Z-Clan Alphas.

That's why I went into the ice water—to mask my scent while I waited for Grey to find me.

I was sure he would come, mostly because my visions had told me he would. But it took far longer than I expected.

However, we're on our destined path now.

Which means we're nearing the fated countdown.

"Didn't you *foresee* his demise?" There's a subtle sarcastic undertone in Grey's voice as he brings me back to our discussion. "I assume that's why you staged everything the way you did with those journals."

My lips twist to the side. "I didn't *stage* anything. I just… tried to help." It's all I can do with my visions of the future. If I explicitly share details of my foresight, then everything changes. But over my last century of life, I've learned that writing down subtle hints can often influence the decisions of others.

When they read my words, anyway.

Something Grey clearly has done.

Because he's here.

*PPS: Our pasts make us stronger, not weaker.*
*Remember that. Remember where you came from.*
*And understand once and for all—you are not*
*him. But sometimes you have to think like him to*
*find the truth. To find... me.*

That was the part of my diary entry I meant for him to see. Fortunately, he did. And, fortunately, we're now here.

Well, unfortunately, too, I suppose.

Assuming my visions of what's to come are correct.

I nearly sigh but busy myself with trying the food in front of me. The moment the flavor hits my tongue, I nearly groan with delight, my insides suddenly clenching with severe hunger pangs.

*Oracle, when was the last time I ate?* I know it's been days. Maybe longer.

I was in Prince Tadhg's "care" for... well, I'm not sure how long. It doesn't matter. He didn't assault me, saying he preferred to let the Z-Clan Alphas do the honors. "You'll be a nice gift," he told me before dropping me off. "Help firm up our alliance."

"I'm glad he's dead," I say softly, not that Grey has actually confirmed it. However, I assume some of the blood he was wearing earlier was from Prince Tadhg. "He was a horrible Alpha."

Grey doesn't say anything for a long beat, then finally replies, "Cillian ripped his head off, then Cael handled the remains."

I try to picture the grotesque scene, but while my mind can depict future episodes, I can't really envision the past. It's strange. But I'm pleased that Grey provided confirmation of the Alpha Prince's demise. "Will Hawk become the new Prince of Alpha Sector?"

Grey shrugs. "I don't concern myself with politics."

I raise a brow at him as I pick up the glass of water beside my bowl of food. "You're second-in-command at Lunar Sector. That seems political to me, Alpha Grey."

"It's just Grey," he corrects me softly. "And I thought you didn't know anything about me?"

"I never said that," I murmur, taking a sip of my drink and setting it down again. "I asked if we could start over with introductions since we'd never properly met. But I do, in fact, know a great deal about you, Alpha."

"Grey," he corrects again. "And pray tell, little riddler, what exactly have you seen?"

My lips twitch. "We both know it doesn't work like that."

"Do we?" he asks, leaning back in his chair. "From what I understand, if you share what you know, it'll change the scope of everything. Does that mean you would prefer we stay on whatever our intended path is?"

And any form of amusement I may have felt… dies.

Because no, I really don't want to walk this path at all.

I know how this ends.

*With me being ripped apart by a pack of wild Alphas.*

I swallow, my stomach no longer desiring any food.

"I'll help you find Nikiski," I tell Grey, aware that's what he truly cares about. Why we're actually here. It's been his mission for years to find his little sister, and somehow, I'm going to help him.

If only I knew *how* I'm meant to help.

The visions are murky. Which is strange because my sight is typically quite clear. However, my destiny with Grey has always resembled a cloud of potential outcomes.

None of them good.

"I assumed that was the point of all your cryptic notes."

My brow furrows. "Cryptic notes?"

"Yes, about the Omega slave trade," he says, his glacial gaze grabbing and holding mine. "You know where my sister is."

"Actually, I——"

He pushes away from the table so suddenly that I stop breathing, my words lost in the now frigid air as he looks directly at the cave wall. "Excuse me," he says, vanishing from sight.

I flinch, my mind instantly recalling all the visions of him *disappearing*.

Leaving me to my fate.

*Choosing her over me.*

My shoulders sag, just for a moment, while I consider what I know will one day come.

Then I shake my head and pick up my water again. *Pitying oneself doesn't fix fate, Ash,* I remind myself. *Consider the positives. You're going to save his sister one day.*

It'll be at a significant personal expense, but that's why fate gave me this gift——to put others first.

Taking a sip of water, I consider what comes next. Then stand and grab another bowl. We're about to have company.

And when he arrives, the countdown will officially begin.

# GREY

"YOU SHOULDN'T BE HERE," I say as I materialize outside of my lair.

Cael stands with his hands in the pockets of his dressy slacks, his dark hair messy and wet from what appears to be a recent shower.

I bet that shower was a lot warmer than my ice bath.

Alas, the blood from the battle in Blood Sector had begun to harden on my skin, making bathing a necessity.

So, when it became clear that Ashlyn wasn't going to vacate my lair's only bathroom anytime soon, I opted for the nearby lake instead of waiting any longer.

"I know," Cael replies, referring to my comment about his presence here being dangerous.

Well, that's not exactly what I said, but it was implied.

"Now let me in," he adds, waving at a nearby rune that's blocking his entry.

It's the same rune that alerted me to his presence mere seconds ago, thus sending a clamoring alarm through my now aching head.

Narrowing my gaze at him, I do as he asks and alter

the rune's magic to grant him access to my lair. The man is practically my brother, his parents having helped raise me after saving me and my mother from my feral father's clutches.

Not a memory I want to relive at the moment.

Yet it haunts my every fucking step.

"Thank you," Cael says, moving into the protective boundary around my safe house—which is actually a cave —and waiting while I re-alter the wards around us.

It's one of my V-Clan gifts that I'm pretty sure are enhanced by my Z-Clan genetics. A unique form of magic, but exceptionally useful. Especially right now.

"Has our little seer provided anything useful yet?" he asks.

*Our?* I repeat in my head. *She's not* our *anything. She's* mine.

Z-Clan wolves are fated.

And this Omega is *my* intended mate.

I've known that from the moment I saw her file in the newly established mating program. It was written in her pretty blue eyes, the way they stared up at me from the screen.

I knew I was looking at my future.

That's why I joined the program—for her.

I assumed she joined for me, too. But it became evident quickly that she was there for altruistic reasons, which she confirmed a bit ago.

However, her comment about me not being part of her choice to join threw me off. I didn't believe her at first, but her clarification made sense.

My little riddler is full of cryptic comments. Yet she's also… truthful. I could see it in her expression, smell it in her scent.

She's not one to lie.

Though, I have no doubt she's one to mask the truth, too. When needed, anyway.

"Grey?" Cael prompts, drawing my focus back to him and the frown he's now wearing.

"She's not *our* little seer," I tell him flatly. "She's *my* little seer."

Both of his dark brows meet his equally dark hairline. "*Yours?*" He huffs a laugh. "Gone a few hours and you've run off and claimed an Omega?"

"There's no claiming required," I mutter. "She was born to be mine, just as I was born to be hers."

He merely shakes his head and releases a low whistle. "I wondered why you joined the mating program. I guess I finally have that answer."

"You've known that answer since the beginning, Cael. Don't pretend like this is news to you." He's the most intuitive Alpha Prince in existence. It's in his blood. In his fucking gifts. "You can't play games with me like you do with others."

"I know," he replies, sounding sad. "Which makes our friendship so fucking boring."

I roll my eyes. "You're an asshole."

"It does make sparring more interesting, though," he goes on, pretending not to hear me. "And goading you even more delightful."

I simply stare at him. "Are you here for something useful? Or just to waste my time?"

"I'm here to talk to our little seer," he murmurs.

My jaw clenches. "You mean you're here to get your ass kicked."

He smiles. "Maybe. Though, I think it would be far more enjoyable for us to go play with some Alphas out here in the Nomad Lands instead."

"I'm trying to mask our presence here for a reason," I remind him.

He lifts a shoulder in a partial shrug. "Well, you don't seem all that interested in letting me speak with said reason, so I was suggesting an alternate activity."

"You're infuriating," I tell him, then grab his shoulder and shadow us into my lair—as there is no door.

"You're perhaps the only Alpha in existence that can get away with insulting me twice in a matter of minutes," he says when my living area comes into view. "Dixon doesn't even press his luck that much."

"I'm not afraid of you, *Your Majesty*." I give him a mock bow, then return to the dining area to find a third bowl of spaghetti already sitting on the table, as well as a chair that Ashlyn must have dragged in from the living room.

She's seated in said chair instead of the wooden one I left her in, her small form dwarfed by the oversized tapestry around her.

"Hello, Prince Cael," she greets warmly. "It's nice to see you again."

"Little seer," he murmurs, his charm in full effect as he walks over to take her hand.

I know what he's going to do a second before he bends, and it takes all my restraint not to go over and rip him away from my fated Omega.

She blushes as he kisses her wrist, the intimate gesture further infuriating me.

Because the bastard knows exactly what he's doing, and he tells me that with a look. His blue-green eyes emit amusement, no doubt noting the fury radiating from my aura.

"Looking for another insult?" I ask through my teeth.

"It's a novelty, to be sure," he replies, taking the seat I

vacated earlier like he fucking owns my lair. "You're usually quite creative with words, Grey."

"No. I'm not," I return, aware that he's still trying to press my buttons.

It's what he's always done.

Hence the reason he's like a brother to me.

Interestingly, though, he never taunts his actual brother, Dixon, like this. They have more of a silent and steady bond.

Meanwhile, Dixon and I have no bond at all. He's never accepted me as a member of the family, let alone a member of Lunar Sector.

Not surprising.

Most V-Clan Alphas loathe my existence.

I'm a hybrid mutt and therefore lesser in their eyes.

What they don't realize is that I mostly take after my mother's side in terms of mental abilities and power. All I inherited from my Z-Clan Alpha father was his size and his strength. *And his feral needs,* I think as I look at Ashlyn.

I witnessed my father's ruts many times throughout my youth.

I have no desire to ever do that to an Omega.

Yet I can feel my beast clawing within me now, demanding that I taste the sweet female sitting in my lair. *Taste and claim.*

Clearing my throat, I force myself to settle into the chair she vacated and reach over to swap the two bowls of spaghetti before Cael tries to eat from my original dish.

But Ashlyn leans forward to swap them back, her eyes meeting mine. "I already knew where he would sit. This was yours from before," she says, setting it down in front of me. "The spaghetti is nice, by the way. Thank you."

"Nice?" I echo, not sure I like that adjective. "If you like it, why haven't you eaten more?"

"I'm not very hungry."

"I already commented on how I feel about lies, Omega," I tell her, certain she's lying now. "You haven't eaten in days. If you want something else, tell me, and I'll make it."

She glances at my kitchenette with incredulity. "I don't think we have many options, Alpha Grey."

The *Alpha* before my name has my beast growling and not because I hate it, but because I *like* it. That's why I asked her to call me *Grey* before. But my little riddler doesn't seem to want to drop the formalities.

*Fine.*

"I can hunt, *Omega* Ashlyn," I say flatly, ensuring she hears the irritation in my tone—both from her choice in using my designated title and her insinuation that I can't satisfy her needs. "Tell me what you want to eat."

Her shoulders fall a little, her gaze lowering to her bowl.

Cael clears his throat. "You've had a rough few days," he says gently, the words clearly for Ashlyn. "I don't want to pry, Ashlyn, but were you hurt at all...?"

She peeks up at him and shakes her head. "No. Prince Tadhg intended for me to be a gift to strengthen his alliance with the Alpha of Kodiak Sector, so he left me untouched and only asked that I deliver a message on his behalf."

"What message?" I interject, wanting to be part of this conversation, not a witness to it.

Ashlyn's lips twist, indicating that she's uncomfortable. "Prince Tadhg sends his regards and hopes you'll enjoy me as a token of his continued appreciation." She utters the words in a monotone voice, then shrugs. "Not very original, if you ask me."

With that, she takes her fork and twirls it through the pasta while I observe her through narrowed eyes.

Any other Omega would be traumatized by the experience she just summarized in a handful of sentences. Yet Ashlyn forces herself to eat instead when I can tell it's more of a trial for her than a desire.

At least I know now that it isn't my food choice that's bothering her, but the general situation. Or I assume that's the case, anyway.

While she's been mostly truthful, she hasn't been all that forthcoming.

*A typical seer*, I think, familiar with the traits, as my sister possessed similar talents growing up. All Z-Clan Omegas have fortune-telling abilities, but their skills vary.

Ashlyn, it seems, is quite powerful.

She's also resilient. Beautiful. *And looking at Cael with far more interest than I like.*

He's smiling at her, amusement dancing in his blue-green eyes.

Clearly, I missed something humorous.

*Did she speak when I wasn't paying attention?*

"You're right, little seer," Cael says, his accent curling around the nickname in a way I strongly dislike. "That isn't very original at all."

*Oh. He's amused by her comment.*

*Fine.*

*Actually, not fine.*

I do not care for him to be *amused* at all.

He glances at me, his eyebrow arching like he's heard me. I wish that were the case. Alas, Cael's mental talents are a lot more complex than simple mind-reading. But he can surely feel the furious energy rolling off my aura.

Of course, in typical Cael fashion, the bastard just smirks and returns his attention to Ashlyn. "Regardless,

I'm glad you're okay, darling. I'll be sure to pass on the status of your good health to Ivana; she was most concerned about your disappearance."

Ashlyn winces. "Yes, please do. I didn't mean to scare everyone."

"Then perhaps you shouldn't have involved yourself in the mating program and played the part of martyr," I mutter.

She and Cael both look at me.

"Without her sacrifice, Tadhg might still be alive," Cael informs me, a hint of dominance underscoring his tone.

"I'm aware of that, *Your Majesty*." I lean back in my chair, not wanting to engage in this foolishness with him. "But she also put herself in jeopardy."

"Which was a bold and dangerous choice," he returns. "And also brave."

"I know." I'm not arguing against any of that. "I'm merely pointing out that if she wished not to *scare everyone*, she should have considered not involving herself in the situation. That's all."

"You're chastising me for a decision that saved countless lives," Ashlyn interjects, her expression fierce as I look at her. "You didn't see the potential outcomes, the future that awaited all of my friends. I will forever sacrifice myself for those I care about, something you would be wise to remember, *Alpha Grey*."

She pushes away from the table, her gaze bouncing between me and Cael.

"I'm exhausted, so I'm going to make this last part brief," she says. "I don't know where Nikiski is, only that I'm destined to help Alpha Grey find her."

Her gaze turns to me, the haunted gleam in her blue depths giving me pause.

"And the 'cryptic notes' in my journal that you

mentioned earlier were from visions I've had of our future together," she tells me. "I've written down what I know. I'll let you know when I see more."

With that, she walks toward the bedroom and shuts herself inside.

# GREY

CAEL RELEASES a chuckle under his breath, the sound grating on my nerves. "I really wish I could stay and watch how this all unfolds," he muses. "Our little seer is a firecracker."

"She's not *ours*," I tell him again.

But one look his way confirms he's just trying to piss me off.

"Yes, the commentary earlier, plus all the growling, made that clear."

"I haven't growled."

"You have," he informs me, his bright eyes glittering with knowledge. "Perhaps not vocally, but the growl was felt." He cocks his head. "It's a good thing I like you too much to accept that challenge from your wolf."

I scoff at that. "I wasn't challenging you, and if I was, we both know I'd win."

One of his dark brows inches upward. "Last time we sparred, it was a tie."

"Because I didn't have anyone or anything to fight for."

I look at the bedroom door. "That's changed over the last month."

"The last month?" Cael echoes, feigning confusion. "Did I fall into a time warp?"

I fold my arms and return my focus to the asshole across from me. "You know Z-Clan wolves are fated. And you know she's mine. So stop trying to piss me off and be helpful instead."

His expression clears, his royal mask falling into place. "I am helping. You just don't realize it yet."

I stare at him.

He stares back.

"I hate your games."

The mask cracks, his lips curling a little into a smile. "You'll love this one, G."

I shake my head. "No, I won't, *C.*"

He lifts a shoulder, then reaches for the drink Ashlyn left for him on the table. It's not water, but a beer from my mini fridge.

And not just any beer, but one from the pack I put in there specially for Cael.

*Clever seer*, I think, suddenly a lot more tired than minutes ago.

"She doesn't know where Nikiski is," I say, grabbing my water—I don't care for alcohol—and taking a long drink. "So we're no closer to finding her." I can't help the subtle hint of bitterness in my tone. Reading those journal entries gave me hope.

I finally thought we might be close.

And now... now I don't fucking know where to begin. *Again.*

Cael sets his bottle down. "She might not know a distinct location, but she's seen visions of where you need to go. Just give her time to share them, and perhaps it'll give you the clues we need."

I dip my chin, agreeing with him even as the bitterness spreads through my veins.

It's not Ashlyn I blame, but myself.

I had one job that night.

One *task*.

*"Grab Nikiski."*

That's all my mother asked me to do.

But when I went into my sister's room, Spruce was there waiting for me.

His lips parted into an evil grin, his green eyes glittering with triumph.

Then he fucking disappeared with our sister in his burly arms, mere seconds before Cael's father shadowed into the compound with his Elites.

My father died horribly that night, a fact that's never bothered me.

But Spruce's betrayal has forever plagued me.

My own fucking brother.

He took Nikiski to the slave trade—to fucking Prince Tadhg—in exchange for a job. Then Spruce died for his trouble.

*Selfish. Fucking. Prick.*

"I know that look," Cael says, his voice dragging me back to the present. "Stop thinking about him."

"He was my fucking twin."

"I know." His vibrant irises run over me. "You got all the good traits; he got all the bad. And he's dead. Let's focus on the one that matters—your sister."

I hate it when Cael is the voice of reason.

I hate even more that I expected him to say *Ashlyn* at the end of that sentence.

Because my priorities are fucking confused.

I've spent a literal lifetime trying to find my sister. I know she's alive. I can feel it in my soul. Just like I sensed when Spruce was killed.

All I've desired is to save her from whatever hell she's currently experiencing. It's all I've lived for.

Until a few weeks ago, when a pair of pretty blue eyes looked up at me from a damn screen.

Fate ensnared me by the knot, and here I am, floundering like a damn pup.

I finish my water and set it on the table, then note that Ashlyn barely touched her food. *Fuck.* I stand without comment and head toward the bedroom, determined to call her back out here to eat. And maybe to apologize.

Because I hadn't meant to chastise her.

However, her disappearance brought back some harmful memories.

And for a moment, I thought I'd lost her, too.

"Scared" was too polite a term for how I felt when I learned about her disappearance.

Still, I shouldn't have commented on her choice of being a martyr.

So, I'll apologize… then coax her to eat.

Only, as I open the door, I realize she's already tucked herself in—robe and all—in the middle of my big bed. Her blonde hair is fanned over the pillows, her lashes resting prettily against her porcelain cheeks.

But there's a lone tear clinging to one of those lashes, the sight of it stirring an ache in my chest.

*Did I put that there? Or did something else?* I wonder, suddenly wanting to slay whatever made her cry. Myself included.

Gritting my teeth, I back out of the room and quietly shut the door again, then turn to find Cael right behind me with an intent expression on his face.

"What are you doing?" I demand.

"Making sure you don't do something foolish."

"Like what?" I ask him, suddenly enraged by his lack of trust. "I know how to respect an Omega, Cael."

He considers me for a moment, nods, and takes two steps back. "I know you do, G. Or you usually do, anyway. But you seem… off your game."

"Off my game," I repeat with a snort. "You play games, Cael. Not me." I move around him, done with this ridiculous conversation. "Don't you have a sector to run?"

"I do," he replies, following me back to the kitchen and watching as I start cleaning everything up. "I also came to give you a present."

"Words of advice?" I guess. "A knife to stab you with?" I look back at him. "Maybe a gun for a new round of target practice, whereby you offer yourself up as said target?"

He huffs a laugh. "Always so creative. And you couldn't hit me, even if you tried."

"I could," I promise him. "I never miss a shot." It's one of my many talents.

He grins. "There's my best friend. Good of you to make an appearance. I was beginning to worry."

I shake my head at him. "You're a fucking menace, *Your Majesty*."

"I am," he agrees, then sets a watch down on the counter.

The sight of it makes me growl.

Cael knows how I feel about metal against my skin.

And while I can concede that the high-tech gadget has its uses, I fucking *loathe* wearing watches.

He knows this.

Just as he absolutely knew I hadn't worn one when I left to retrieve Ashlyn.

Hence the reason he's brought me one now.

*Fuck.*

"Wrong on all accounts, I'm afraid." His words are light, poking fun at my guesses while trying to tame my reaction to his *gift*. "I know you hate them, Grey, but it'll help you keep me informed on your progress. Plus it's added security."

I grunt. "I can handle myself."

"While I agree, I think we both know this is the smart play—for her." He glances at the bedroom door.

Like I need to know who he means.

Or maybe I do.

*Her* could also apply to Nikiski.

Maybe it applies to both.

I don't fucking know, but I'm extremely unamused by this "gift" of his. Being practical is a moot point. I don't have to like it just because he's right.

"Alternatively, you could bring our little seer back to Lunar Sector, if you prefer," he murmurs.

I narrow my gaze. "Refer to her as *ours* one more time," I dare him.

His grin grows into a full smile. "Good luck, Grey. And try not to be too hard on *our* little seer, yeah?" He disappears before my fist can meet his jaw, the bastard's chuckle a residual echo in the air that has me growling in annoyance.

"Asshole," I mutter, aware that I've called him that more than once this hour.

The watch lights up with a message, creating a translucent screen above it. I snort when I read the note as it appears one word at a time. *Love you, too, brother.*

I know he hasn't bugged my lair. He just anticipated my insult.

Because he knows me well. Too well, in fact.

A sigh leaves me, and I focus on finishing up in the kitchen. Ashlyn is going to need something better to eat tomorrow. Something nutritious and filling.

Too bad all I have are canned and boxed goods in the pantry. I rarely ever visit this safe house, keeping it stocked with just the essentials—like water for me and beer for Cael.

Maybe I'll go for a run in wolf form and see what I can catch. Or fish in the pond out back.

I grab the back of my neck and stretch, my body far tighter than it should be.

A shift could be good.

I'll just have to ensure my presence isn't sensed by anyone nearby. Or maybe go several miles away for my run so I don't lure anyone back to the cave.

*Hmm.* I stretch my arms over my head, then go check on Ashlyn again. She's still tucked into a ball, sound asleep in my bed.

It's the only one in this lair.

Which means we're going to have to share it.

Fortunately, it's big enough for us both.

But I can't join her in my current mood. I need to run off some steam.

*So a run it is,* I decide, pulling off my shirt and laying it on my couch as I return to the living area. My pants and boxers follow.

Fully naked, I find a notepad and a pen to write a note for Ashlyn—letting her know where I've gone—then grab Cael's *present* and shadow to a nearby tundra. The terrain makes it easy to spot potential threats. The terrain could also be useful for "losing" this precious piece of metal.

Alas, Cael is right.

So I slide the damn thing onto my wrist and growl as

the magical metal melts into my skin. It feels like a damn noose around my neck, reminding me of a previous life.

*Of a collar that suffocated my aura.*

Growling, I engage my shift, aware that the device will transition with me. Fortunately, it doesn't throttle my powers. It just... aids them. A different kind of tech.

My white paws touch the earth a few seconds later, my wolf eager and ready for a sprint.

So I let him go.

Enjoy the wind in my fur.

Free my mind.

And simply... *exist.*

# ASHLYN

Silence greets my ears.

*Eerie* silence.

I felt Grey leave, his presence a blanket of security I already miss.

*Will he be back?* I wonder, shivering as I curl tighter into my robe.

I know the answer is *yes*.

Because we have seven days before the mayhem begins.

Seven days before my world ends.

Seven days before his life begins again.

My stomach clenches, the prophecy swirling through my mind as a myriad of chaotic visions assault my mind.

It's strange knowing what will come to fruition, yet not knowing exactly how it will all unfold. My foresight is usually clearer than this. Alas, all I *see* are the same gruesome fates.

Tomorrow, I'll share a few key details with Grey, see if anything sounds familiar to him.

For now, all I can really do is try to sleep... and to dream.

*I hate dreaming*, I think, shivering again, but for a very different reason this time. *But for Grey... I'll dream. I'll embrace the nightmarish images, search for important clues, and do what I can to guide him.*

Because I meant what I told him—I will always sacrifice myself for those I care about. What's the point of possessing a gift if I can't use it to help those I love?

And while Grey and I may not know one another well, my heart and soul have cared about him for a very long time.

Since the first instance when he appeared to me in a dream with those alluring eyes.

*My fated mate.*

*My destiny.*

*My intended end...*

Another tear falls from my eye, the treacherous display of emotion making my stomach twist. At least Grey didn't notice. Or maybe he did, but couldn't be bothered to provide comfort.

That's fine.

Sometimes, I hear him purr in my dreams.

Maybe this week, he can purr for me in reality.

I would like that. It might make the pain worth it in my final hours.

Sighing, I wipe the dampness from my cheek and snuggle into the pillow with traces of Grey's evergreen scent. The hint of snow is missing, suggesting it's been a very long time since he lay here. But that's okay. It's enough to calm my aching heart.

For now, anyway.

My inner wolf feels different, her deep cry a sound of mourning, like we've already lost our Grey.

But he'll come back this time.

He has to.

It's the only way for this dance with fate to truly begin.
That knowledge is what chases me into my sleep.
Where I dream.
Of death.
Destruction.
*And desolation...*

# GREY

I LEAN AGAINST THE DOOR, watching Ashlyn sleep.

She has barely moved in the last twelve hours, not even while I rested beside her.

Well, that's not entirely true.

At one point, she curled into my side, which caused a purr to ignite in my chest.

A purr I couldn't quite quell.

After ninety minutes of trying, I finally forced myself to leave the bed and go take a long shower. But Ashlyn remained in that tiny ball the entire time I was gone, her head on the pillow I vacated.

I run my fingers through my damp hair, the droplets falling onto my bare shoulders. I'm not in the mood to wear a shirt today, the fabric feeling a little too tight for some reason.

So I settled on a pair of gray sweatpants instead.

If the shirtless thing bothers Ashlyn, I'll find something else to wear. But I suspect she won't care. She's a shifter, after all. Nudity is pretty common for our kind.

Yet I can't help but admire the sliver of skin peeking out from the part in her robe. The curve of one breast is visible, the skin appearing creamy and soft.

If she were truly mine, I would trace that exposed part of her with my tongue.

Alas, we've barely even touched.

*Outside of sleep, anyway*, I think.

My leg still burns from where her thigh rested over mine. It took considerable effort not to move toward her, to seek out the heat radiating from her core.

Clenching my jaw, I push away from the door and force myself to go grab a water from the fridge. The contents are half gone when I hear a soft whimper come from the bedroom.

Brow furrowing, I set the bottle down. *Am I—*

A sharp cry radiates through the lair, sending me racing toward Ashlyn. She's no longer curled into a ball, but writhing in the sheets like she's trying to fight someone off.

Her arms swing and she growls, thrashing violently against the pillows.

Then, just as abruptly, she curls into herself and whispers, "No. No, please. Please don't. I... I don't want..." Another scream rips from her lungs, the sound piercing my chest like a fucking bullet.

"*Ashlyn.*" I start toward her, only for her screams to turn to sobs. "*Fuck.*"

"Grey..."

"I'm here," I tell her, rushing to her side.

But she's not awake. Her eyes are still closed as tears stream down her face. "It's worth it," she says.

"What is?" I ask, utterly confused by this conversation and what's happening right now.

"Fate… is worth… the pain." She curls even more tightly into the fetal position, her head tucked against her knees as she begins to violently shake.

"Fuck this," I breathe, my purr igniting as I slide into bed with her and pull her into my arms. "Wake up." It's obvious she's having some sort of nightmare. A vision, maybe. But I don't fucking care. She needs to… "*Wake up.*" A growl underscores those two words, my animal *demanding* that she obey.

Our Omega comes alive on a gasp, her body going rigid, then falling into a fit of trembles once more. I hold her tight, my purr louder than it's ever been.

"You're safe," I tell her. "I'm here."

And Ashlyn practically melts into me. "A dream," she mumbles against me. "*A dream.*"

"That didn't seem like a dream, Ash," I mutter, the nickname rolling right off my tongue. "That looked more like a nightmare."

She stills, then pulls back a little to look up at me. "Wait… I'm… I'm awake?" Her voice sounds a bit hoarse, probably from the screaming seconds ago.

"Yeah, little riddler. You're awake. And you're safe." I keep purring for her, my hand automatically rubbing her back —a gesture that seems to cause her to curl into me even more.

I accept it.

In fact, I'm pretty sure I love it.

But that's… that's a consideration for later.

Instead, I just hold her. Purr for her. Give her the strength she needs to fully rouse from whatever hellish vision made her cry like that.

Her face is still wet, dampening the skin of my chest as she buries herself against me.

It's like she's trying to escape into me somehow, or

perhaps get to my purr. I'm not quite sure, but I keep the rumble going as her breathing begins to even out and her body relaxes. She's not asleep, just... soothed.

"Thank you, Alpha," she whispers.

"*Grey.*"

She giggles a little, and the sound is almost drowsy. "Thank you, *Grey.*"

I smile because there was a hint of sass in that reply.

"Most Alphas prefer to be addressed by their titles," she adds, her voice softening.

"With anyone else, I might prefer it, too. But I need you to call me Grey."

She tilts her head back, and her eyes look impossibly bluer, maybe from her tears. "Why?"

"Because calling me *Alpha* awakens my beast," I tell her honestly. "And you're not ready to meet him yet."

Ashlyn studies me for a long moment, the sadness seeming to slowly dissipate from her features. "I'm very familiar with beasts... from my nightmares." Her words sound like a confession. Though, I'm not quite sure what she's truly confessing.

"Are they visions?" I ask.

She nods, her white-blonde hair glinting from the low lighting in the room.

"Related to my sister?" It's a hard question for me to voice, but I need to know.

When Ashlyn nods again, my heart stops.

"You can see her?"

She shakes her head then. "No. I... I can't really see her, just feel her. Like I am her at times."

My stomach clenches, thinking about what she's saying.

*The writhing on the bed.*

*The screaming.*

44

*Ashlyn saying she doesn't see my sister, but she is my sister... at times.*

"Like this dream you just had?" I press, my voice barely recognizable.

Her brow furrows. "Er, no, not quite. It... it was a combination of visions. Cause and effect." Her lips twist. "It's hard to explain, and I can't voice too much without risking a change."

"Given how much you were screaming, I think a *change* might not be a bad thing."

She swallows, the movement slow and purposeful. "In my experience, changes are never for the better."

My chest aches with the thought. "I don't know what you're seeing, but if that's happening to my sister—"

"It's not," she interjects. "That... It's related, yes, but not her." She closes her eyes and takes a breath. "Give me a moment, please. I'm still trying to process, and I'm struggling to explain."

The pain in her voice has my purr reigniting in an instant. I didn't even realize I'd stopped. But the moment I begin again, her shoulders seem to fall and she leans into me, like she needs more of my rumble.

So I give it to her, my hand resuming the caress against her back as my mind tries to puzzle through everything she's saying.

I thought she meant those *beasts*—the ones she was clearly fighting in her nightmare—were hurting my sister. Whether it be now or in the future.

But she just said that's *not* happening to my sister.

*So who is it happening to?*

Her words while she slept come rolling through my mind. *"Fate... is worth... the pain."*

That doesn't sound like it's related to my sister at all, but to Ashlyn.

"Are the beasts attacking you in the vision?" I ask, aware that she just requested time to process everything, but needing to know if I'm understanding her fear.

The way she stiffens again confirms what I need to know.

"Visions are complicated," she replies, not at all answering my question.

"Ashlyn—"

"I can't, Grey," she whispers, sounding exhausted despite having slept over twelve hours. "It's delicate. I... I don't want to make anything worse by revealing too much."

"Then give me something to work off of," I demand. Because I can't let that happen to her. I can't let that happen to Nikiski. I just can't let any of it happen.

She sighs and drops her head back once more. Her eyes are less frightened than before as she meets my gaze.

"Whenever I dream of her, there are endless candles. I've always wondered why, but..." She looks around at the walls. "I suppose you would need a lot of candles if you lived inside a cave, right? Because there would never be any sunlight."

Her words are a riddle, yet not.

"You think she's in a cave."

Ashlyn shrugs. "I don't know for sure. But I think it's possible, yes."

"That's not very helpful," I admit, sighing a little.

"Perhaps not," she agrees, sounding sad again. "However, I would think a massive cave system might stand out on a map. Especially one with that many candles."

I frown. "How many candles?" That seems to be an important note.

"Thousands," she whispers. "Thousands upon thousands."

"I see."

Her lips curl, but it's not a happy smile. "Pretty sure you don't, Alpha Grey. But that's why I'm here, right? To be your eyes?"

"*Grey*," I growl at her.

She shivers in response. "Grey," she echoes, her palm coming up to caress my cheek. "You should know that it's not your beast I fear in my nightmares, *Alpha*. I'm not afraid to meet him."

*Fuck*. My inner wolf snarls in anticipation, ready to give her exactly what she desires. Which I am *not* doing. Particularly after whatever hell she just witnessed in her sleep.

"You need to eat," I grind out, needing some manner of sanity to latch onto. "I'll make you some salmon."

Her eyes widen. "Salmon?"

"Didn't *see* that coming, hmm?" I muse, my palm still caressing her back. "My beast likes to play in the water."

"So you went ice fishing?"

"Sad I didn't show you how to properly fish?" I counter, recalling the Glacier Sector incident again. That was what she and Alpha Henrik were doing when she fell in. "I thought that was *Henrik's* responsibility."

Amusement chases away the residual sadness in Ashlyn's features. "He wasn't a very good teacher."

"Shocking," I deadpan.

She giggles, the sound one she's made twice now in my presence. And I find I'm rather fond of it.

"Next time, I'll take you with me."

Her gaze brightens. "Really?"

"If you want to learn, sure." I shrug. "I don't mind teaching you anything you want to know."

She seems to sit up a little straighter. "Anything?"

Okay, now I'm intrigued. "Is there something you want me to teach you?" I ask, curious as to what has her looking at me with such eagerness in her pretty eyes.

"Runes," she says, shocking the hell out of me. "I know you make them for protection. I would love to learn how to do that, too."

"I…" I frown. "I'm not sure that can be taught." Runes are layered with magic, and she's a Z-Clan Omega. She has foreseeing abilities that are clearly quite impressive, but what I do requires V-Clan genetics.

"Can you show me anyway?" she asks, hope a bright emotion in her alluring features.

"If that's what you want, yes," I tell her. "I'll show you whatever you want, Ash."

Her cheeks pinken a little, probably from the nickname I've just used for the second time. But she doesn't remark on it. "Thank you."

"You can stop thanking me," I murmur. "Actually, no. If you want to properly thank me, you'll eat something."

She releases a laugh this time. "Okay."

"Good." I hold on to her for another beat, then force myself to set her to the side. "I'll be in the kitchen. Join me when you're ready. You'll eat… and I'll teach."

Her responding smile is so fucking beautiful that my heart aches. "You have no idea what this means to me."

I don't. But I can see it means a great deal by the way she's looking at me. "I'm not a normal Z-Clan Alpha, Ashlyn. I believe in respecting Omegas. I hope you believe that and understand that."

"I do," she says, her expression sobering a little. "More than you know, Grey."

There's a hint of something in her tone that I can't quite identify, no doubt linked to some vision or another.

48

So I don't overthink it or analyze it further. Instead, I give her a nod. Then head toward the kitchen and prepare to feed her.

*Protective runes*, I think, frowning a little. I haven't mentioned them to her, but she clearly knows I have a talent for them. From a vision, perhaps?

But the real question is, *why does she want to learn how to make them...?*

# ASHLYN

I DRAW my finger through the air, just the way Grey showed me three days ago.

But nothing happens.

*Ugh.*

He's supposed to be my fated mate. I was hoping that I might be able to, I don't know, tap into his V-Clan powers somehow.

Queen Quinnlynn does that with King Kieran.

Ivana and Cillian also share impressive abilities between them.

So, why not me and Grey?

Maybe because he hasn't claimed me, nor I him.

But I know Queen Quinnlynn was able to use some of her mate's powers after their initial engagement to one another. Although, that did require a bite…

*Hmm.* I'm not sure if that's possible with Grey and me.

And, as a full-blooded Z-Clan Omega, I might not be able to tap into his magical talent, either. But it's worth trying, right?

Grey shadows into the cave with a bucket in his hand and walks into the kitchen.

*Naked.*

My eyes are instantly drawn to his strong thighs and ass, my mind seeming to blink off in an instant.

*He's naked.*

*Why is he naked?*

*Because we're shifters.*

*Right.*

*Holy knot...* I can't stop staring. *He's getting hard.* I should stop staring. *Oh, wow, he's large. Very long. Thick.* I really need to... to not... *Knot...*

*Pretty sure I've swallowed my tongue.*

*Yep.*

I've seen all types of shifters without clothes. But never one quite this beautiful. Or muscular. Or *endowed.*

"Ashlyn?" Grey's deep rumble has my gaze tracking up his defined torso to his square jaw dusted with dark blond hairs.

"Hmm?" I hum, a little lust-drunk by the perfect male specimen in front of me.

I've never desired an Alpha before. Which makes sense, as I always knew I was destined for *this* Alpha in particular.

But I didn't realize I would be this consumed by his presence.

He frowns at me, the action one I only notice since I'm still staring at his chiseled jawline.

Grey starts to walk away, and I observe happily, noting the way all his muscles flex deliciously with his movements.

Then I pout as he pulls on a pair of gray sweatpants.

*I was enjoying that view, thank you,* I think sourly at him. *Oh well.*

Sighing, I continue my task of attempting to create a rune.

Still nothing.

"It's a V-Clan trait," Grey says, returning to the kitchen to wash his hands.

"Yes, you've said that," I murmur. "Doesn't mean I can't try, though."

He glances at me over his defined shoulder. "Is there a reason you want to know how to create protection wards? I already have several up around this cave."

I shrug. "It seems like a useful skill." It's a vague response. But I don't want to elaborate on why these might be helpful in my future. "I can't exactly take down Alphas physically, so developing a mental ability seems a more appropriate route."

"And what Alphas do you intend to take down?"

I glance at him, confused for a moment. Then realize I uttered that last part out loud. "Oh, I don't know. But I'm a Z-Clan Omega. Knowing how to defend myself is a natural need." Not a lie. Not the full truth either.

*Why did I voice that last bit out loud?* I wonder, giving myself a shake.

Sometimes talking to Grey is a little too easy.

Which is why we need a subject change.

*Um...* "Can you tell me more about Nikiski?" It's the first question to scroll through my mind, and I almost immediately regret voicing it.

Only, I actually would like to know more about her. More about Grey. More about their past.

"Maybe it'll help me understand my visions," I explain out loud, feeling a bit like a floundering dolt.

*I blame the knot,* I decide. *Grey should not flaunt that impressive specimen in my presence. It clearly alters my brain chemistry.*

*As well as other things...*

He stares at me like I've lost my mind.

Probably because I'm acting erratically.

But I'm a seer. This sort of inane behavior should simply be accepted. Especially by a Z-Clan Alpha. Or, er, a hybrid one. Whatever.

"Please," I say, needing him to speak again. Anything to shut up the babbling in my head.

He grabs a towel to dry his hands and turns to lean back against the counter, his long legs crossed at the ankles as he studies me. "What would you like to know?"

"Anything." There's a hint of desperation in my tone that I wish wasn't there. But I can't help adding, "Everything."

He folds his arms across his chest. "Do you know why I live in Lunar Sector?"

"I know your mother is a V-Clan Omega," I tell him. "So I assume it has to do with that."

He nods. "About a century ago, during the height of the Infected Era, Cael's parents were trying to round up missing Omegas. My mother was one of them."

That makes sense. During that period of time when the zombielike plague was ravaging humans, supernatural powers were also shifting. Sectors were being created. Alliances made. *Omegas taken…*

My visions during that period were… unpleasant. The slave trade began then, or rather, found renewed strength. Alphas trading Omegas wasn't a new concept, but many Omegas were displaced during the upheaval. And certain monsters chose to take advantage of that.

Monsters like Prince Tadhg.

"My father was taking us all back to Kodiak Sector," Grey goes on. "He couldn't shadow, so we traveled on foot."

I frown. "Why didn't you just shadow them?"

"Because my father had me collared," Grey says flatly, the words making me wince.

"He throttled your abilities," I translate.

"With a literal collar," he replies. "Yes." He glares down at the watch on his wrist. "I've never been a fan of metal on my skin as a result."

"Then why wear a watch?" I wonder out loud.

"Cael," he mutters. "It's a safety measure."

"Oh." My nose scrunches. "Could I, uh, wear it for you?" It's an awkward question, and the watch will look ridiculous on my wrist, but if it makes him feel better, then it's worth offering.

He looks at me in surprise. "What?"

"If you don't like the sensation of it on your wrist, then I can wear it… when we're together, I mean."

His brow furrows a bit. Then he shakes his head. "It's okay. I can bear it."

I shrug. "Just an offer, if you need it."

"Thank you." He swallows. "I'll keep that in mind." The sincerity in his tone tells me he means that.

His arms fall to his sides, his hands slipping into his pockets as he stares at me for another beat.

Then he clears his throat and continues his story about his family's trek across Canada to Kodiak Sector.

"Cael's father found me somewhere in Alberta," he says, a faraway glint in his icy gaze, like he's reliving the memory. "He nearly killed me."

"That wasn't very nice of him."

Grey grunts. "I was a hybrid Z-Clan and V-Clan Alpha mutt in his eyes. But when I couldn't fight back—because of the collar—he stopped his attack and told me to start talking."

He goes on to tell me what he said to Cael's father, how he begged the Alpha to help his family escape his father.

"I didn't care what he did to me so long as my mother and siblings were safe," he mutters. "But for some reason, he chose to save me, too. Basically became the father I never knew I needed."

"Where is he now?" I wonder out loud. "Still in Lunar Sector?"

He nods. "Cael's whole family is there. My mother, too. But Cael proved to be the superior Alpha, so his father relinquished the Prince title to his son."

"That would never happen in Kodiak Sector," I mutter. "Or any of the Z-Clan sectors."

Grey huffs a humorless laugh. "No. No, it would not."

Z-Clan Alphas tend to kill their young if it seems like the offspring might pose a threat to the hierarchy.

It's deplorable.

Monstrous.

*Horrific.*

That's why his father's collar doesn't shock me. He was trying to tame his strong son. Had Cael's father not intervened, it's very likely that Grey would have one day been killed by his own father's hand.

"Anyway, the night his father came to rescue us all, it was my responsibility to grab Nikiski. But Spruce got to her first."

My shoulders stiffen. "Spruce?" I echo, the name one I've heard in my dreams. Though, I'm not sure when or how. It's... it's foggy. But I know that name.

"My twin," Grey growls. "He took Nikiski and bartered her life for his own—to Tadhg."

"You're certain?" I ask, somewhat confused by this description of events. Because something about it doesn't sound right to me. Though, I can't... I can't explain why.

"Yes." He pushes off of the counter and comes to sit across from me at the table, then tells me about his research with Cael, how they followed the messy path left behind by Spruce, which took them to Alpha Sector. "We've spent nearly a century trying to decipher every avenue of the network, but there have been a lot of false leads and dead ends."

"Tadhg?" I ask.

"Gave us basically nothing," he mutters. "His two sidekicks weren't of much use either."

My lips twist. "Sorry." I hoped they would garner something important from the situation, but my true goal had always been to protect the Omegas. And that, at least, was a success.

"Don't apologize for something you can't control," he replies, sighing. "Tadhg was one of the main supporters of the organization. That much we know with certainty. But we're still trying to determine who is running the show."

"Because you think that person has your sister," I assume out loud.

But he shakes his head. "No. We just want to kill everyone involved." He says it lightly, yet I know he means every word. "Our next move—in terms of organization—is to set up a meeting with the Gold Sector Prince."

My eyebrows lift. "The dragons?"

He nods. "We think they're involved, or at least know something of importance. Cael is working through his channels to arrange it."

"Why not just call Prince Oros?" I ask, confused. "Be blunt."

"You're familiar with the dragons?" he counters, leaning forward. "You've *seen* them?"

"Not really, no. But I've been around long enough to be familiar with their royalty," I reply. "There's also a Drakon-Clan Omega in the Sanctuary. He's quite insightful."

He stares at me. "He?"

"A male Omega, yes. You know they exist."

"Yes, I do. But now I'm curious about why this male Omega is *insightful*."

"Would it make you feel better if it were a female Drakon-Clan Omega?" I ask, teasing him now. "If I called *her* insightful?"

His jaw visibly clenches. "Why is *he* insightful?"

"Because he knows a lot about the world," I tell the simmering Alpha. "And he was just a friend, *Grey*. So calm your beast." I purposely only use his name, not his title, to try to get through to him.

Though, I won't lie, I rather like the possessive energy rolling off my fated mate right now.

I'm not even sure he's aware of it.

Or maybe he is, but doesn't care.

He pushes his chair back and stands, then leans down to place his palms on the table, his gaze capturing and holding mine with an intensity that makes me stop breathing. "The next time you want to mention one of your *insightful* male *friends*, remember it was *my* knot you were salivating over mere minutes ago. *Mine*."

With those unexpected yet profound words, he steps away and stalks off toward the bedroom.

"Your knot is the first one I've ever seen," I call after him. "And the only one I've ever desired."

He freezes on the threshold.

"I'm not a virgin, Grey," I add, standing and staring at his back.

He turns slowly, his nostrils flaring.

"Not in the strictest sense, anyway," I go on. "But that's only because I've required relief during my heats. And there are toys that simulate a knot—while *alone*—in a nest. However, none of those simulators compare to the one between your legs. So, hopefully, knowing that helps calm your beast."

He simply stares at me.

And I stare back.

"I've known my fate since my very first heat," I go on. "I'm not sure if that's fate's way of ensuring an Omega remains untouched or not, but in my case, it did. I've never felt the need to dally, knowing who would one day come for me. Thus, jealousy isn't necessary. At least, not on your part regarding my prior *friendships*."

Grey doesn't appear to be breathing.

I wait for him to say something.

He doesn't.

And I suddenly feel very foolish for admitting everything I just said.

It all sort of came out.

He doesn't like lying, which means he prefers honesty. So why hide from our destiny? He knows as well as I do that our souls are linked.

I've just known about it longer.

"Right. Sorry. I've had a century to prepare for this. I understand that you need more time to process it." Which is truly heartbreaking, honestly, as we don't have much time to spend together before the end.

However, he doesn't know that.

And I can't share that detail with him, either.

It'll change fate to something worse, and given how horrific it already is, I hate to fathom what *worse* could actually mean.

Clearing my throat, I take a step toward the bucket he left on the floor. "I'll... I'll clean the fish," I mutter, needing something to do. "Get it ready for dinner."

Silence meets my words.

For once, I wish I could *see* what might come next.

But I can't.

Because, as with most things involving Grey, it's *cloudy*.

One would think being a seer might come with certain advantages. However, the only advantage I seem to have is when it comes to helping others. Never myself.

Suppressing a sigh, I pick up the bucket and set it by the sink, ready to begin.

Only, my hand is caught before I can reach in to grab a fish. I glance back at Grey, confused, and suddenly find myself pinned between him and the counter as he spins me around to face him.

"What—"

His mouth comes down on mine, the kiss so surprising that I forget how to breathe.

How to think.

How to *exist*.

Because my Alpha—*my intended mate*—is kissing me.

*And I never even saw it coming…*

# GREY

## A Few Seconds Earlier

ASHLYN'S CONFESSIONS were so unexpected that I fucking froze.

She's a virgin.

Because she knew her fate.

She knew *I* was her fate and didn't let anyone touch her.

What am I supposed to do with that knowledge?

My beast is roaring with victory inside me, demanding that I charge forward and take what's mine.

*Fuck.*

The way she looked at my knot when I shadowed back in here... It was like she wanted to go to her knees and acquaint herself personally with my cock.

Only now I want to kneel for her. Pleasure her. *Thank her.*

*Because she waited for me...*

Every possessive instinct I harbor is both appeased and inflamed by that realization.

63

I watch as she picks up the bucket and sets it by the sink, her movements stiffer than they should be.

But I don't even care what she's trying to do or what she said about cleaning the fish.

All I want to do is *devour* her.

I don't walk into the kitchen; I shadow there, grab her hand before it can touch the contents of the bucket, and spin her around.

Her blue eyes blow wide, confusion crossing her features.

I don't give her a chance to comment or question me. I simply do what I've wanted to do since the moment we first met.

I kiss her.

And I don't kiss her nicely, either.

I kiss her with a passion that's been brewing since the moment I learned of her existence.

She thought I needed more time to process this.

Fuck, she couldn't be more wrong.

I processed and accepted it the second I locked eyes with her photograph.

Some Alphas fight their fates. I have no desire to waste time. And I show her that with my tongue. Let her taste me. *Truly* know me. Feel my interest. My *desire*.

She's soft. Beautiful. Intelligent. Altruistic.

I would be insane not to want this. Not to want *her*.

Releasing her hand, I reach up to palm her nape and pull her closer. All she's wearing is one of my T-shirts, the fabric hanging around her like an oversized dress.

I know there's nothing underneath it, a fact that has my dick throbbing in response.

I'm hard.

Pretty sure I've been hard since she stared boldly at my knot.

"Fuck, Ashlyn," I breathe against her mouth, my beast raging inside with intrinsic need. Controlling him will be impossible soon.

And I... I'm not sure what will happen when I let him go.

That's the feral part of me that I fear. The one that's far too similar to my father.

Thinking of him reminds me of her note, the postscript she wrote about how I'm not like him.

She couldn't be more wrong.

There's a viciousness inside me that longs to be set free.

That Z-Clan compulsion to *destroy*.

I don't want her to ever meet that feral part of my nature.

And I can't trust my beast not to introduce her to it.

Not yet, anyway.

Maybe not ever.

Though, she said my beast wasn't the one she feared. *What did she mean by that?*

It's a question I lose track of as her hands meet my abdomen, her palms burning against my skin as she slowly caresses my torso. Exploring. Learning. *Stroking.*

A little moan of pleasure escapes her, causing me to reach down and grab her hips. I need her even closer, but this height difference between us is making that difficult.

I lift her into the air, and her legs automatically wrap around my waist, her arms going to my shoulders.

And suddenly it's like we were always meant to be this way—her body cradled against mine as I carry her to the bedroom.

This is moving fast.

But I don't fucking care.

This female was meant to be mine. *And she waited for me,* I marvel again. *Fuckkkk, she waited...*

What I don't tell her is that I waited, too.

I've been with a handful of women, but never an Omega. I saved my knot for my intended. I worried I might never find her, that perhaps my V-Clan genetics had altered my destiny, but still... I held back and never embraced any other opportunity.

So knowing that Ashlyn did the same...

I lay her out on the bed and crawl over her, my lips seeking hers once more.

*Perfection.*

I pin her to the mattress and ravage her with my tongue.

*Mine.*

My cock throbs as I settle between her thighs.

*Omega mate...*

I've never felt so off-balance, yet stable, in my entire existence.

She feels incredible beneath me, so soft and warm. I palm her cheek, needing to keep her lips against mine as I explore her with my opposite hand.

Gently at first.

Testing her boundaries.

Identifying any limits that might exist.

Tracing her arm, noting the goose bumps pebbling against her skin.

Stroking her shoulder and then down her side, my thumb brushing her plump breast in the process.

Never once does she stiffen. If anything, she just goes more placid against me, like she's *melting* into my touch.

And maybe she is.

"Did you foresee this?" I wonder out loud, my voice a whisper against her mouth. "Do you know what comes next?"

She shakes her head, causing her nose to bump mine.

"N-no," she stammers, her big blue eyes looking up at me. "I've never… you've never… in my dreams, I mean."

I frown. "I've never what?"

"Kissed me," she says, sounding far more shy than in the last few days.

I pull back a little. "I never kissed you in your visions?"

She shakes her head again. "No."

"Did I knot you?"

Her pupils dilate. "No…"

This doesn't make any sense. I go to my elbows on either side of her head, needing to understand. "We're fated." Not a question, but a statement.

"Yes."

"You know we're fated."

"Of course."

"And never once have you dreamt of me kissing you?" I demand.

"Not once." Her eyes go to my mouth. "But I've thought about it before."

I arch a brow. "Not as a vision, just a… fantasy?"

Her cheeks pinken. "Yes."

*Hmm.* I study her features, liking the way the pink turns redder with each passing beat. "What did you fantasize about?"

Her eyes widen. "That's private."

"Says the female who was openly ogling my knot back in the kitchen," I drawl. "Tell me what you want me to do to you, Ash. If you share, I might reward you by making the fantasy come true."

This will help me know how far to take this.

And it gives me better control over my beast.

He's quiet inside, waiting for her response.

She says nothing for so long that I think she's going to ignore my request. Then finally her light-blonde eyelashes flutter, and she looks up at me again. "Can I show you instead?"

"You can do whatever you want to me," I tell her honestly.

A wicked little glint enters her gaze. "I'm not sure you should give me that power."

"Do your worst, Omega," I dare her, then roll off of her to lie on my back and tuck my hands behind my head.

Her expression shifts into one of wonder, almost as though she can't believe I'm letting her lead. Then she gingerly crawls over me to straddle my hips. There's no mistaking my intrigue, my cock pushing against the sweats to settle right against her pussy as she situates herself on top of me.

The little flare in her nostrils tells me she noticed.

And the way she moves a bit against my shaft suggests she likes it, too.

The oversized shirt hides her curves, but I see the subtle hint of her nipples protruding against the fabric. She's interested.

Which is also evidenced by the dampness I feel seeping through my pants.

She's aroused.

*Slick*, I think, wanting to push up into her. *Gods, I want to feel that against my cock.*

No, I want to *taste* it on my tongue.

I've never had the pleasure. Never experienced an Omega's tight cunt. Always waiting for my intended—for *this*.

Yet all Ashlyn has done so far is straddle me.

She's studying my torso, her hands at her sides.

"You can touch me," I say, inviting her to play. "In fact—"

My wrist begins to buzz, and I nearly jump out of the

bed, the reminder of the metal against my skin instantly killing my mood.

"*Fuck.*"

It takes me a moment to remember how to breathe, the vibrations reminiscent of another time... of a collar choking me whenever I tried to shadow...

Ashlyn strokes my arm, drawing my attention back to her. She's frowning, but not at me—at my watch.

Because a screen has appeared with Cael's name scrolling across it.

He's calling me.

Which isn't like him at all.

Sighing, I grab Ashlyn by the hips and pull her off of me. I can't talk to him while she's straddling my cock, especially with her slick permeating the air. "I'll be back after I talk to him," I tell her.

A strange little expression crosses her face, one I can't quite read. "Yeah, okay. I understand." Something about that reply strikes me as off, but I'll address it after I make the buzzing stop around my wrist.

I lean in to brush my lips against hers. "We'll revisit your fantasy, too," I promise her.

Then I shadow outside of the cave and accept Cael's call.

"What?" I demand, unable to hide my impatience.

His eyebrows fly upward in response. "What Omega has your knot in a twist?" He feigns an epiphany in the next moment. "Oh, that's right. *Ashlyn.* How is our little seer, hmm?"

"Do you want me to hang up on you?" I ask him.

"Do you want me to call again?" he returns.

My jaw grinds, my irritation mounting. "You know I hate metal against my skin, Cael."

"I do. But you need that device for safety."

"Then don't use it for random phone calls," I tell him. *Especially when they interrupt an intimate moment with my Omega,* I nearly add.

"This isn't a random call. But you answered with so much politeness and poise that I haven't had a chance to enlighten you on the purpose yet."

I roll my eyes. "Stop wasting my time, *Your Majesty*, and spit it out."

"'Stop wasting my time,' he says," Cael parrots at me, shaking his head. "If only you knew."

"*Cael.*"

"My, but she really does have you all tied up, doesn't she?" Cael muses, and I move my hand up to hit the Disconnect button. But then he adds, "I'm calling about Oros."

My hand returns to my side. "What about him?"

"We have a meeting set for a little under two hours from now. Virtual. Do you want to join?"

"Yes," I say without hesitation. "But I assume that means you need me in Lunar Sector." Because I won't be able to join securely from here. The watch is powerful and useful. Alas, it has limits.

"It does," he admits. "However, it should be a brief discussion."

I nod. "All right. I'll resecure my runes here, then come in just for the call."

As much as I would love to take Ashlyn with me, I can't. If her presence is felt or even suspected in Lunar Sector, then I'll have to answer to a trio of powerful V-Clan Alphas that I really don't want to deal with right now.

Cael's expression says he feels the same. Still, he asks, "Will she be safe there?"

"Temporarily," I reply. "But I can't be gone for long."

"We'll time it," he says. "Tell me what you're

comfortable with, and you can leave if we reach that limit."

"I'll talk to Ashlyn about it, see what she prefers." I don't want to leave her here unprotected or without any concept of when I'll return. "If she's not comfortable, though…"

"Then I'll handle the call alone and provide you with a summary."

I nod.

"But, Grey," he says, a note of seriousness in his tone. "He mentioned needing to share important information about a new Omega acquisition. He told me to be prepared to *accept* his declaration, whatever the fuck that means."

I frown. "You don't think it's related to Nikiski, do you?"

"I don't know. Oros is impossible to read."

"Most Drakon-Clan Alphas are," I mutter, running my fingers through my hair as I try to interpret the cryptic information. "Gold Sector has a lot of caves, right?"

"I believe so, yes."

"With candles?" I ask.

He shrugs. "I haven't visited that area of the world since the Pre-Infected Era, so I honestly don't know what the Greek Isles have become. Other than dragon-ridden, of course."

I sigh. "Yeah, all right. I'll talk to Ashlyn."

"Good. Let me know if you're not coming; otherwise, I'll see you in"—he looks at something off-screen— "ninety-eight minutes in my office."

The screen goes black, signifying the end of the call.

I shake out my wrist, mostly to make the translucent magic retract into its metal casing, but also because I need to reassure myself that the watch isn't a collar.

With a mental grimace, I shadow back into the cave and find Ashlyn right where I left her.

If only I could join her again.

"You need to eat," I say, heading into the kitchen. "And we need to talk."

# ASHLYN

My stomach twists.

Because I recognize what's about to happen. I've *seen* it before.

Not the kissing. Or the writhing in the bed. Or the feel of Grey's big hands on me.

But this moment—the one where he tells me he has to leave.

It's the beginning of a sequence of departures, all of which lead to the same end.

Swallowing, I fix my shirt and leave the bed, all the while ignoring the dampness between my thighs. He felt it. He knows I'm aroused. Or that I was, anyway. There's still evidence of it on his sweatpants.

However, I can't muster the energy to be embarrassed about it. Nor do I think I should be embarrassed. I'm an Omega. He's my Alpha. Of course I'm aroused around him.

I join him in the kitchen and watch as he cleans the fish —the very ones I was going to clean before he grabbed me and kissed me.

Alas, he's clearly not thinking about that anymore.

"What do you want to talk about?" I ask, already knowing the answer.

"Gold Sector."

My brow furrows. "Gold Sector?" That's not… that's not what he was supposed to say. *Why is this moment changing?* I wonder, glancing around to make sure I have the right scene. *Or maybe—*

"They have caves. Underground tunnels." He glances at me. "Do you think that could be the vision of all the candles?"

I blink at him. "I… I don't know. It's possible?"

"Have you seen any gold or any dragons in your visions?"

"I…" I frown. "I don't think so."

He looks disappointed.

So I feel compelled to ask, "Why?"

"Oros, the Prince of Gold Sector, agreed to that meeting with Cael. But he added some cryptic commentary about an Omega acquisition that he wants to tell us about."

"Oh." My nose scrunches because none of this matches my expectations for this moment. It feels all wrong.

*Why haven't I envisioned this?*

Or is this utterly unrelated?

"I was wondering if it could be related to Nikiski," he goes on, his gaze still on me. "Any feelings or thoughts on that?"

"I… no," I admit. "But I think you should probably attend that meeting to hear him out." Because I want more information now on what I've missed.

My seeing abilities are usually much more accurate than this.

"It'll require me to go to Lunar Sector," he says.

I nod. "Yes, that makes sense."

"I would take you with me—"

"But you can't because Kieran or Lorcan will shadow in to take me back to the Sanctuary. I know," I interrupt, very aware of this part.

Because *this* we've discussed in my head.

However, the cause for why he needed to go home was much different.

*Unless this is leading to him finding Nikiski?* I wonder, then shake my head. "Yeah, no, you have to go. I know you do. That's fine. I'll be okay here." *For now,* I nearly add out loud. Instead, I step away and say, "I'll help you make this lunch or dinner or whatever it is, then you can eat before you go."

"Ashlyn," he says.

But I'm ignoring him and grabbing things from the fridge.

"*Ashlyn*," he tries again.

When I don't instantly respond, he takes hold of my wrist.

A shock rolls up my arm, his touch electrifying.

I meet his gaze. "Grey?"

"I'm coming back," he tells me.

It takes everything inside me not to wince. Because those words haunt my nightmares.

"*I'm coming back*," he always says.

Only, he doesn't.

He doesn't come back at all.

"Hold on," he murmurs, turning to the sink to wash his hands.

I watch him, not sure what he's planning to do. Because, again, this isn't something I've foreseen. Everything is so muddled. So *strange*.

*Gold Sector?* I think, still trying to process that potential shift in location.

None of my predictions have involved dragons, only ever wolf clans.

But if the dragons are involved, that could explain some of the fuzziness in my sight. They're mystical creatures, similar to the V-Clan wolves. Only, their powers are less known outside of their various sectors.

*Could a dragon be messing with my visions?*

"All right," Grey says, facing me again as he dries his hands. "I'm going to draw a protective rune on you. It'll be one that's linked directly to me as well, so if you have any issues, you can use it to alert me."

I blink at him in confusion. "I thought runes were for inanimate objects."

He smiles, the motion showcasing part of a dimple on the left side—one I've never noticed before. "Many are, but there are a few that work in this manner."

He steals the items from my hands—ones I forgot that I took from the fridge—and sets them on the counter. When he takes hold of my wrist once more, another wave of electricity dances along my skin, making me shiver.

I'm again at a loss for what's about to happen. And it's both unnerving and thrilling.

His eyes are kind as he stares down at me, the softness new.

*Because we kissed?*

I swallow, sort of wanting to forget all of this and just kiss him again.

His tongue felt like velvet against mine. Dominant. Soft. *Addictive.*

I want to experience so much more from his mouth. So much more of *him.*

He draws his finger along my inner forearm, tracing

the veins up from my wrist. "Are you going to watch so you can try to learn later?" he asks me, his voice holding a touch of amusement.

"You think I'm crazy for wanting to learn how to make runes," I mutter. "But other mates share gifts, you know."

His touch stills, and I realize I've just given something away. Not intentionally. Nothing drastic. Just *why* I wanted him to teach me.

"Will you inherit my talents when we mate?" he asks, studying my features. "Will I inherit yours?"

"I don't know," I admit, my heart beating a little faster.

He said *when*.

*When we mate.*

*Does that mean…?*

*No.*

I squash the thought train entirely. I *know* that will never happen. Not the way he's insinuating, anyway.

"It's a silly desire," I tell him, trying to brush all this off. "I just thought it might be fun to know how to do… if it ever happens."

"It's not silly at all," he replies, his thumb caressing my wrist. "So pay attention. This design is a little trickier since it's on the skin."

He starts slowly, showing me the pattern and explaining the angles. It's basically like learning a foreign language, only with lines and dots, not words.

But I focus on everything he says, doing my best to commit the design to memory. It helps that it's actually glowing on my skin, almost like a fiery tattoo.

"Will it stay like this?" I ask when he's done, admiring the sharp edges and knotted pattern.

"Until I remove it, yeah," he replies. "So if you need me, you just have to press your thumb here." He grabs my other hand and uses it against the golden pattern sketched across my skin.

When my thumb meets the heart of the design, a soft hum stirs in the air. It's kind of like an alarm, but not loud. Just a presence that can be felt.

"You sense it, right?" he asks.

I nod.

"Good." He releases my arm but brings my hand up to his lips to press a kiss against my palm. "All you have to do is touch the rune like that, and I'll feel the same energy buzz."

I blink at him. "I've never seen any of this." It's a confession, one he seems to understand.

"Then perhaps we're altering fate—in a positive manner," he replies, leaning down to brush his lips against my cheek. "Now, I have about sixty minutes left to cook, eat, and recharge the protective wards outside. So let's work on lunch next."

"Lunch?" I echo, wanting to confirm the time. Because it's been a little weird living in a cave.

He glances at me. "When I get back, we'll go for a run. I'm sure your wolf would like some exercise."

"But it's lunchtime?" I press.

"Yes."

"So the sun is out and high in the sky?"

His brow furrows a little. "Yes." He faces me again. "Why?"

"Just curious," I say, shrugging. "It's been a while since I saw the sun." That's not a lie. But it's not the truth either.

Deep down, I'm concerned.

Because night is when bad things happen.

If it's sunny… then maybe I'll be fine. Maybe he really will come back.

Clearing my throat, I ignore my racing thoughts and focus my energy on helping him in the kitchen. It's our fifth fish meal of the week. *Good thing I've spent the last few decades on an island in the Arctic,* I think. *Otherwise, I might be sick of salmon already.*

Grey doesn't say much as we eat, but I can feel him scrutinizing me. I've revealed a lot more than I ever intended to reveal today. So he might be right about changing fate.

I really hope he's wrong, though.

By the time we finish, he needs to leave. So he quickly changes into a pair of jeans and a black sweater, then comes back into the kitchen after putting on some boots.

I force myself to smile as I say, "See you soon."

He studies me for another beat. "Remember the rune, Ash." He draws his finger over it, like I may have forgotten about the glowing symbol on my arm. "If you need me at all, *call.*" He presses his lips to my temple, the intimate gesture stirring butterflies in my stomach.

Then he shadows out of the cave.

I know he's nearby still, just *recharging* the wards, as he said. But I can't sense him.

Instead, I simply feel alone.

In a cave.

*Where I'll eventually meet my doom.*

My stomach clenches with the thought, my eyes falling closed. *No point in dwelling, Ash,* I tell myself, then shiver when I hear Grey's voice in my head calling me by the same name.

The nickname was unexpected, and again, *unseen.*

But I like it.

I open my eyes once more and focus on the kitchen. It's a mess again.

*Might as well clean it,* I decide, craving a distraction.
Afterward, I'll take a shower.
Then I'll wait for Grey.
And see if he actually comes back.

# GREY

## LUNAR SECTOR

I wish I could say it felt good to be home.

But it doesn't feel good at all.

In fact, I've been here for five minutes, and I'm ready to head back to the Nomad Lands.

I palm my chest, hating the strange ache growing inside. I know Ashlyn is my fated mate. However, this sense of longing is highly inconvenient.

Cael casts me an amused look, his gaze bouncing between my hand and my face. "Missing our little seer?"

"Did you call me here for a meeting or a sparring match?" I counter. "Because I'm leaning toward the latter."

His lips curl. "In the century I've known you, I don't think it's ever been this easy to goad you."

"I haven't slept well these last few days." Not a lie. I've been hard every fucking night and consumed with the need to purr for Ashlyn while she dreams.

It's intrinsic nature to just hold her and provide

comfort. I'm not even sure she's aware of any of it. But she has to know we've been sharing a bed. There's nowhere else for me to sleep other than the floor or the love seat in the living area.

Cael looks ready to reply, when his monitor lights up with an incoming call.

The humor disappears from his features in a flash, the Alpha Prince on full display in less than a blink. I stand across from him, not planning to show my face or reveal my presence yet.

"You're not Oros," Cael says, his dark brow inching upward. "Onyx, I presume?"

Silence meets his question, and I suspect it's due to a moment of surprise. "Most outsiders don't know the difference between me and my brother."

"I'm not most outsiders," Cael replies, his voice holding an edge to it. "I'm also not a fan of bait-and-switch dynamics. So unless you have something important to say, I'll be hanging up now."

"We're both here, Prince of Lunar Sector," a cultured tone murmurs, the owner of which I assume is the *brother*—Prince Oros. Both men have accents, the English inflections seeming to be tainted with something else. Romanian, perhaps?

"I don't enjoy games," Cael informs them, causing me to nearly snort out loud.

Because that is a bald-faced lie.

I don't comment, though, not wanting to distract Cael from his *game*.

"My apologies," the cultured tone says, not sounding apologetic at all. "My brother and I share dominion in Gold Sector. I may be Prince, but he's just as powerful as I am."

"Sometimes more powerful," the other one comments. "I'm also very protective."

"A trait I can admire," Cael inserts. "But I would rather get to the point in this discussion. You mentioned an Omega acquisition?"

"Are you not the one who desired this call?" Onyx counters, his voice holding an edge to it that helps me identify the speaker. His brother might be the prince, but it's clear that Onyx is the harsher of the two. I'm betting that's why Oros is the diplomat and Onyx is the second-in-command.

"I desire information on the organization hosting the infamous *hunting parties* throughout the world." Cael's sharp tone carries through his office, his wolf peeking out through his blue-green eyes. "I believe you're familiar with it."

"That is the rumor, yes," Oros inserts smoothly. "Gold Sector has an intimidating reputation to protect, similar to the elusive V-Clan wolves."

Cael frowns as he watches the screen, making me wonder what he's seeing.

"Yes, please," Oros says, his voice suddenly much softer than before.

*Please what?* I think.

"That's fine, *printesa mea*," Oros murmurs. A shuffling sound echoes from the speakers, and Cael's eyebrows shoot upward. "I want you to meet Prince Cael of Lunar Sector. His second-in-command is hiding somewhere else in the room and rudely has not appeared yet."

I roll my eyes.

"Grey, I believe," Oros goes on. "Yes?"

Cael looks at me.

I look back.

Then I shake my head and move around to stand

behind my best friend. "Yes" is all I say, but inside I'm shocked at what I see on the screen.

The Gold Sector Prince has an Omega in his lap.

And she's not dressed in chains, though she's certainly wearing a lot of gold. But she's in some sort of black dress... and she's *smiling*. "Hello," she says, her voice soft and sweet.

"This is my Omega acquisition," Oros murmurs. "Otherwise known as Taliana, my new queen. I thought you would be interested in seeing her since I believe she's part V-Clan wolf. But I'm not actually sure, as her genetics are mixed."

"Which is the point of our call," Onyx goes on. "If you want to learn more about the infamous organization you mentioned, you need to look into Obsidian Sector."

"That's where Taliana is from," Oros adds. "Her father brought her here for sanctuary and—"

Onyx looks up sharply, as does Oros.

Then Onyx curses. "Excuse me" is all he says before disappearing in a cloud of silvery specks.

"Did Mari just...?" Taliana whispers, her voice carrying through the speakers.

"I think so." Oros sounds amused. But then he clears his throat and looks at Cael. "Onyx is right about Obsidian Sector. We should talk more."

"More than we are now?" Cael asks.

Oros smiles. "Let me rephrase—we should talk in person. You're welcome any time, *Prince Cael*." His gold eyes peer up at me through the screen. "You, too, Grey."

The screen goes black before either of us can reply, and Cael releases a low growl. "Fucking dragons."

"You don't like games?" I ask, unable to help myself.

He turns slowly to glare up at me. "I don't like games with dragons."

"Seems to me that you and Oros might have a future together at a chessboard," I say conversationally. "Invite me to the match. I want to watch."

"So you can cheer him on?" Cael guesses.

"Absolutely," I reply.

Cael just shakes his head. "You're a shit friend," he accuses, his accent thickening.

"Pot, meet kettle."

He snorts. "Obsidian Sector?" he asks, abruptly changing the topic back to what the dragons said.

"The only thing I know about Obsidian Sector is that they enjoy hunting in the Nomad Lands of former-day Europe." I fold my arms. "But maybe we should go snooping."

He nods. "I'll talk to Dixon, see if he can help us map it out."

His brother is good with technology and reconnaissance, so I agree with a dip of my chin. "In the interim, I'll be with *my* seer."

I don't give Cael a chance to comment, just shadow right back to the cave and find Ashlyn in the kitchen.

She shrieks upon seeing me and drops the pan in her hand. "You're back?" She frowns. "Or you just finished the runes?"

I chuckle. "I'm already back from the meeting."

She blinks at me like she's confused. "But you were gone maybe twenty minutes?"

"It was a quick call," I tell her. "Have you ever dreamt of Obsidian Sector?"

She simply gapes at me. "What?"

"The dragons said we need to look into Obsidian Sector and its links to the shadow organization managing the Omega slave trade."

"Oh." Her nose scrunches. "No. I honestly don't know

anything about Obsidian Sector, but I'll consider it and see if I can find any links during my next vision."

She returns to cleaning up the kitchen, but I can tell by the tightening of her shoulders that something's bothering her.

I'm not sure if it's related to the dragon or my abrupt return.

Or something else entirely.

She's definitely hiding things from me, though. Secrets about the future. I understand her hesitation to share, but… "When we mate, I'll have access to your mind." The words leave my mouth before I can stop them. However, they're true. "So anything you *see*, I'll also see. How does that impact the future?"

Ashlyn finishes scrubbing the dish—which appears to be the final one to clean—then washes her hands before facing me. "Honestly, I don't know," she says quietly. "A lot of this is unexpected, and I'm struggling to understand why."

"Because you didn't see it?" I ask, ensuring I understand what she means.

"Yes, exactly that. I—"

The hairs along my arms dance mere seconds before an alarm blares through the cave.

Ashlyn's face goes white. "You said it's daylight," she whispers.

"It is," I reply, frowning at her.

Then the energy heightens, causing my wolf to growl.

"We need to go." I grab Ashlyn and engage my shadowing gift, but nothing happens. No dematerializing of the room. No darkness. Just… standing still in the cave.

*What in the hell…?*

I release Ashlyn, and my arm instantly starts to disappear. I stop the shadowing transition, though it feels a little sluggish, almost like it's my first time trying to teleport.

"What just happened?" Ashlyn asks, confusion and concern etched into her features.

"I can't shadow you," I tell her. "Why can't I shadow you?"

"I don't… I don't know. You shadowed me in here…"

"I did." And it felt fine. I also just shadowed in here myself. "Something weird is happening."

I can sense it in my detonating wards outside, the zaps of electricity echoing through my veins.

"We're going to have to do this on foot."

Ashlyn gapes at me. "But there's no door."

"That's not quite true," I mutter. "We can tunnel."

"Tunnel?"

I don't respond to her echoed question. Instead, I head toward the bathroom, to the small escape hatch I built into this safe house long ago.

There was a time when I couldn't shadow or do much of anything at all. A time that taught me how to rely on my physical strength alone.

While I despise that part of my life, it also framed who I am today and how I built my various dens.

"I always have a plan in place in case someone manages to collar me again," I confide to Ashlyn.

The only other individual in the world who knows that is Cael.

"We're going to have to crawl," I warn her as I remove a vent cover. "And the space will be a bit tight." I look down at her petite size. "More for me than for you."

Her blue eyes are wide, but all she does is nod. "Okay."

I look over her T-shirt. She's going to freeze outside.

"Can you shift into your wolf to crawl? Or will she be

too big for the tunnel?" I move to the side so she can see the space for herself.

"I would prefer to be in human form," she tells me.

"It's going to be cold, Ash."

"I'm not afraid to freeze." She utters the words with conviction, and I wonder if she's thinking about her time on the icy shores of Kodiak Sector.

However, there isn't time to ask. The urgency dancing along my skin tells me we need to move. Because more of my wards are firing off warnings.

In all different directions.

Anything could be coming for us right now. Wolves. Vampires. *Dragons.*

It's hard to know for sure. The runes just notify me of approaching predators, not the type. But the number of flares shooting off in my head tells me it's a pack of intruders, not a solitary one.

Fortunately, my wards are doing their job in providing a distraction.

I can almost feel the grenade-like explosions rippling through me. Only, they're miles away at the moment.

That gives us just enough time to escape on foot.

*Or a snowmobile, anyway,* I think as I move into the tunnel to lead. Ashlyn follows without a word, her sweet scent filling the space and adding a renewed sense of importance to the equation.

"When was your last heat?" I ask as we move, my question soft yet riddled with underlying wariness.

I should have inquired about that on day one.

"Too long ago," she says quietly. "I knew not to imbibe anything in Glacier Sector, so I didn't experience the forced estrus like many of the others."

I wince, aware that several Omegas went into a forced heat after what Granger did to them.

But I wince even harder at the realization that Ashlyn might go into heat soon.

"I should have taken you back to Lunar Sector," I mutter, annoyed that I let a potential confrontation deter me from properly protecting Ashlyn.

"I'm where I'm supposed to be," she answers calmly.

Which means she's foreseen this chase already.

That explains her lack of fear right now. Most others would hate being in this tight space, not knowing where it leads.

But not Ashlyn.

She's trusting the process and perhaps is already aware of where we'll end up.

I don't say anything else for a while, just crawl quickly through the tunnel system I created decades ago. It's what allows fresh air to enter the cave but also serves as a decent escape hatch.

By the time we reach the end, my wards have almost all blown up, but the chaos is unfolding behind us, not in front of us. I can sense that my runes ahead are still very much enabled and alive.

Which is good, as I don't feel like fighting our way out. It'll be a waste of precious ammunition.

I push the grate out from the wall ahead of me and hear it fall with a clang against the cement below.

Grabbing the sides, I hoist myself through the opening and perform a tuck and roll onto the floor before jumping up to my feet. Then I turn and pull Ashlyn through the opening so she doesn't accidentally fall forward into the pitch-black space.

Of course, her eyes should be as adjusted as mine to the darkness.

But I don't mind the excuse to touch her.

I set her on the ground, then reach up to cup her

cheeks. "I'm going to find you a coat, gloves, a scarf, and some boots. They won't do much, but they're better than this shirt."

And she's going to need the layers for the snowmobile ride.

"Afterward, I'll need you to wear a backpack full of supplies," I tell her.

She says nothing.

"Okay?" I prompt.

"Yeah," she whispers. "I've just never *seen* this before."

I frown, following what she means. "This isn't in your visions?"

"No." She swallows, and I hear it more than see it. "Where are we going?"

"I'm not sure yet," I admit. "But we'll find something."

There are emergency bunkers hidden all over this region of the world, most of them built by humans during the Infected Era. The majority are energized by solar power, a technology that's easily reconfigured, even if it's a little rusty.

I go grab the supplies we need—including the items for Ashlyn—and bundle her up. Then I guide her over to a tarp that I rip off to reveal our ride. It's already gassed up and ready.

"Do you have escape huts like this attached to all your lairs?" she asks, sounding impressed.

"Yes." Survival is one of the skills I've mastered in my lifetime. "One can never be too cautious in this world."

"Always preparing for alternate paths," she says. "I'm beginning to understand why we're fated."

"Only beginning to?" I ask, grabbing her nape and pulling her toward me. "You haven't *known* all along?"

"Not everything can be revealed in visions," she breathes, her head angled up toward mine.

"Hmm," I hum, then lean down to kiss her softly. "We'll see what else we can *reveal* after we find a new den." I nip at her bottom lip, then pick her up and settle her on the snowmobile.

Grabbing a helmet with a face shield, I put it over her head and ensure she's protected. Afterward, I help her with the backpack and put a few items—mostly guns and ammunition from my emergency stockpile kits—in the various storage areas on the vehicle.

I slip into a leather jacket lined with fur and use a rubber band to tie my hair up into a bun at my nape.

The last thing I retrieve is a pair of gloves, the waterproof material easily gliding over my fingers and hands as I secure the items in place.

"All right," I say, sliding into place in front of her and picking up my own helmet. "Wrap your arms around me, Ash, and don't let go. This is going to be a dangerous ride."

# ASHLYN

## NOMAD LANDS, CANADA

WE'VE BEEN DRIVING for hours, the sun having set ages ago.

Of course, it's that time of year when the days are shorter than the nights. So it's hard to know exactly how long we've been on this snowmobile. But it's clear that Grey wanted to put a lot of distance between us and his cave.

The howls piercing the air as we left told me why.

There had to be at least a dozen wolves, if not more, trying to find us.

Which shouldn't have happened for another two nights, by my count. But my visions have proved to be inaccurate where Grey is concerned. And he did utter the infamous words that were supposed to initiate my future hell.

Yet now I feel a little lost. Confused. Elated. And scared.

Because I have no idea where this path leads.

All my visions are of going into heat in that cave and being ripped apart while Grey saves his sister from the candlelit cavern.

Not only am I not in heat at all, but I'm... I'm also no longer in that cave.

So nothing is what it seems, again suggesting that something or someone has been influencing my visions. *But how? Who? And why?*

The dragons tend to keep to themselves, just like the wolves. Our dynamics are vastly different. Wolves are pack creatures, choosing a hierarchy based on strength. Or, with V-Clan wolves, based on mental abilities.

But the dragons... they structure their authority based on bloodlines. They're purists by nature. There's power in blood, and they form their alliances accordingly.

*So why manipulate my mind?* I wonder as the snowmobile finally begins to slow. *What's the endgame?*

For once in my existence, I can't see it. I can't see anything at all.

And that terrifies me.

"Recognize any of this?" Grey asks as he kills the engine.

"No," I tell him. "Nothing at all."

"Is that good or bad?"

"I don't know," I admit. "I... This has never happened to me before."

He places his hand on my arm—which I barely feel, as I'm basically an ice cube now—and gives it a squeeze. "We'll figure this out together, Ash."

"Okay." I have to clamp my teeth together to keep them from chattering. It's like now that we've officially stopped, the chill is catching up to me. I've been forcing myself to ignore it this entire ride, focusing instead on my mind and trying to envision what's to come.

But I'm mentally blind. No hints. No paths. Just the present—which is a clearing of trees with what appears to be a cabin in the distance.

"I'm going to go check this out and see what's inside," he says, giving my arm another squeeze. "I want you to stay here and keep your hands on these bars, then drive if you hear anything or anyone coming that isn't me."

I try to nod in agreement, but my body is a little too stiff. I'm not sure I could drive even if I wanted to. "O-okay," I manage to force through my teeth.

He glances back at me, the action one that I only notice because he moved his head.

We can't really see one another clearly through the face shields, the mirrored outer layer instead reflecting the moon overhead and the surrounding snow.

Grey removes my arms from his torso and slides off the snowmobile, then takes off his helmet. Mine disappears next, allowing us to meet each other's gazes. His reminds me of a black hole in the ice, his pupils so large that there are only thin glacial rims around them.

Without a word, he takes the backpack from me—an item I stopped feeling hours ago—then lifts me into a bridal hold and carries me toward the cabin. "I don't hear any heartbeats or smell anyone," he says softly. "So the property is vacant. But those panels on top tell me it's been fashioned for solar energy."

I swallow, my teeth now chattering freely as I can't seem to clench my jaw anymore.

"We'll make do and stay here for the rest of the night," he goes on. "Then continue on in the morning."

I want to ask how far his snowmobile can go on whatever tank it has, but I don't have the energy. So I just angle my chin a little to acknowledge what he said.

Then I lay my head on his shoulder and close my eyes, exhaustion overwhelming me.

Maybe it's the cold.

Maybe it's the lack of sight.

Or maybe it's… it's just life.

However, I'm suddenly too tired to do anything other than breathe. Exist. And curl into his heat.

I'm not sure when I start to thaw, or when the world begins to warm up again, but it feels like I go from being an icicle to a flame in a matter of minutes.

Except… except, when I open my eyes, I find myself naked in a cocoon of blankets.

*With a naked man holding me.*

My eyes widen, the windows before me showcasing a winter wonderland lit by the sunrays above.

*What…? Am I dreaming?* I wonder. *Is this a… a vision?*

No, it feels too good to be a picture of the future.

So a dream is more likely.

Or a fantasy, even.

Because I can feel a *knot* against my rump. It's hot. It's hard. And it's part of an even harder shaft.

*Grey,* I think dizzily, a moan nearly escaping me. *A very naked Grey is holding a very naked me.*

A shiver works through me despite the heat blanketing me from the inside out.

This is the best dream of my life. I never want to wake up. I simply want to exist in this moment forever.

But the wall behind me begins to move, a rumbling purr vibrating my back.

I sigh, deciding this is my personal heaven. "Please don't stop," I whisper.

"Why would I stop?" Grey asks against my ear, clearly awake. Er, awake in my dream, anyway. Which I already assumed, given that his erection is branding my ass.

Plus the purr.

I don't think Alphas purr whilst asleep.

Or maybe they do.

Regardless, he's very much aware in my dream right now, which means I can indulge.

"Will you kiss me?" I ask my Alpha, wanting to see where this goes.

He presses his lips to my shoulder, then my neck. "Like this?"

"Yes," I whisper, arching back into him. "But more." I roll toward him, my palm finding his cheek. "Kiss me like I'm yours."

"You are mine, little riddler," he murmurs. "My fated Omega." His mouth brushes mine, softly at first. Sweetly. Then his tongue parts my lips, and passion ignites between us.

I grab his shoulders, loving how strong and hot they feel beneath my palms. Almost like he's *real*.

He rolls me to my back, his lower half settling between my thighs as he masters me with his tongue.

It's intense.

It's hot.

It's better than I could ever have imagined.

Especially with his weight on me. His bare skin against mine. His cock hard against my clit.

I push up into him, not caring at all that he can feel my arousal. It's not like he's hiding his.

And this is my fantasy, after all.

I may as well do what I want. Enjoy the embrace. *Experience our mating...*

I dig my nails into his muscles, earning me a growl from the Alpha. A growl that's mixed with his purr. The sound is delectable and draws a moan from deep within.

I want so much more.

His knot inside me.

His thick shaft stroking me.

*His teeth in my skin…*

"I wish you could truly claim me," I pant against his mouth. "Make me yours in every way… for real." I lean in to kiss him more, but he pulls back to stare down at me.

"Why wouldn't I be able to claim you?" he asks, his brow furrowing as some of the lust leaves his features.

"Because this is a dream," I tell him, laughing a little. "But if you want to bite me, I won't say no. In fact, I think I would like that a lot." I tilt my head to the side. "It would be nice to know how it'll feel. A memory to take with me to the grave."

He stills. "What does that mean?"

Now it's my turn to frown. "What does what mean?"

"A memory to take to the grave."

I sigh. "Can we get back to the kissing and claiming thing? This feels like a waste of time, especially when I could wake up at any moment."

He goes to his elbows on either side of my head. "Ashlyn."

"Grey," I murmur coyly back at him, then bat my eyes. "Bite me."

"No."

"What do you mean, *no*?" I demand. "This is *my* dream."

"Ash—"

"If you're not going to bite me, then at least knot me. That's the least you can do after everything I intend to endure for you."

He gapes down at me. "And what is it you intend to *endure* for me?"

I stare up at him, my lips curling down into a deeper

frown. His question doesn't feel right. Because it's not something I would ask myself in a dream.

In fact, I wouldn't be doing *any* of this in a fantasy. Just kissing and knotting.

But the way this Alpha is studying me... doesn't feel all that fantastical. It feels real. *Too* real.

"This isn't a dream," I whisper, realizing the truth of it as I voice the words out loud.

"No. It's very much *not* a dream. So start talking."

I shake my head. "I can't."

"You can."

"No, Grey. I *can't.*"

"We've already changed the future. You told me you couldn't see anything else. So why not tell me what you thought was going to happen and let me help you move on from there," he says, his tone carrying the weight of his Alpha authority.

"It could still happen." I shiver with the thought but take in the surroundings again with a frown.

None of this is familiar.

None of this feels *destined*.

"How long was I asleep?" I ask him, another thought occurring to me. "How many days has it been since Cael's visit?" Because maybe... maybe everything is still going to happen, just in a new place.

That could be the change.

The alternative path.

*But how am I going to protect myself in this open cabin with glass windows that overlook a forest clearing?* I wonder. *Unless there's a cellar or a bunker underground...*

"Why?" Grey demands.

"Why?" I echo, not following. "Why what?"

"Why do you need to know how many days it's been?"

*Oh.* My nose scrunches, then my teeth clench together as I glare up at him. "Because it's important."

His eyes narrow. "Tell me why."

"Tell me how long it's been," I counter, my heart beginning to race when I realize that today could be the day everything changes.

I look outside again, needing to see the sun. It might be my last time ever seeing it. Because once nightfall comes...

"Please tell me how long it's been," I whisper, unable to hide the tremor in my voice now as the visions begin to assault my mind.

The horror.

The blood.

*The grunts...*

"Grey, I need to know... I need to know how long it's been. *Please.*" I can't stop the tears from filling my eyes, terror taking hold of my throat and making it impossible to breathe. *If it's tonight—*

"Eight days." His words interrupt my thought, the response not making any sense. "We traveled well into the night after leaving the lair, almost to morning. Then you slept for two days. Cael visited on our first evening in the cave, so eight days."

I blink.

Then blink again.

"That..." That doesn't make any sense.

The seventh night is when it all happens.

"You're sure?" I ask, my voice a choke of sound due to my lack of air.

"Positive," he says, then lifts his arm to show me his watch.

Which reveals a date.

The date honestly means nothing to me, given that I

rarely pay attention to calendars. I rely on visions and serendipitous occurrences to guide my concept of time.

But I can't *see* anything.

Not anymore.

*Eight days.*

*That's impossible.*

Only, maybe not.

We're on an uncharted path now.

I…

I don't know how to feel about that. I don't know how to *see.*

"Ashlyn."

*What am I going to do?*

*What happens next?*

*What if—*

"*Ashlyn,*" Grey snarls, his wolf seizing hold of mine in a vise that forces me to look at him. "You're safe. I'm here. And we're going to figure this out together."

More tears fill my eyes, my literal vision going blurry.

"The first thing you're going to do, Omega, is breathe for me," he tells me, his voice underlined with dominance.

It's a dominance I can't ignore.

A dominance that forces me to *obey.*

My lungs burn as I inhale, the pain echoing through my nerve endings and making me shake.

"Good girl," he praises me. "Keep breathing."

I do.

And that agony starts to subside.

"Now," he says, a purr in his voice. "We're going to get up and take a shower together because the generator is working and we have hot water."

*Okay*, I think, unable to speak.

"Afterward, we're going to eat," he goes on. "And then, we're going to talk this through."

All of that sounds… scheduled.

Too scheduled.

I… I don't really want to be *scheduled*.

I want to exist in the moment because I don't know if it's our last. I don't know what happens next. I don't know if we're even going to survive.

It seems foolish to waste our final moments on showers and food and words.

Not when there's so much we haven't yet experienced together.

So I find myself shaking my head.

"No?" he asks.

"No," I echo, the words more mouthed than anything else. Because my throat feels raw.

But I don't care about that.

I care about this. I care about him. I care about *us*.

I force my head up off the pillows and press my lips to his, all while holding his gaze. It's a challenge. A dare for him to stop me. A plea for him to *take me*.

His palm wraps around my throat, his thumb brushing my pulse as he gently pushes me back down.

I'm about to protest, to *beg* him to give me what I need.

But then he kisses me again.

This time with dominance.

Power.

*Precision.*

His tongue masters mine in a skillful dance that makes my thighs clench around his hips. This is a kiss of intent. A kiss of understanding. A kiss that grounds me in the present and forces me to ignore the future.

*Yes,* I think. *Yes, this is what I need to survive whatever hell awaits us tomorrow.*

I wrap my arms around his neck and cling to him, desiring his strength.

Our eyes are no longer open. Or, at least, mine are closed. It doesn't matter. All I care about is his touch. The way he continues to hold my throat is an unspoken declaration of power.

I'm his.

My life is literally in the palm of his hand.

I trust him implicitly, my soul having been his for a very long time.

But he's never truly been mine. Until now. Until *this* moment in time.

It might be fleeting. However, I'll make sure it's enough to satisfy my heart and my mind for whatever nightmare awaits me.

"Ashlyn," he murmurs against my mouth, his opposite hand grabbing my hip.

Only then do I realize I've been gyrating against him, bathing his cock in my slick while seeking friction for my core.

It was so natural.

So *intrinsic.*

Yet I'm not in heat. Not quite, anyway.

Which is also strange because I should be.

But I don't want to think about what all of that means or why my estrus hasn't arrived yet.

I really don't care to think at all.

"Please don't stop," I say, repeating the words I thought I'd whispered in a dream. Except it was real. *This* is real. "Please give me this, Grey. A moment where we can be *us.* It's... it's all I've ever desired. For myself."

The tears are back again, and I hate this show of weakness.

However, if he knew the horrors in my mind, he would understand. He wouldn't even hesitate.

"If I knot you, I'll claim you."

"Then claim me," I tell him. "Make me yours, just as fate intends me to be."

He shakes his head, but it isn't in denial. I can see the wonder in his features. As well as his wolf.

He's about to lose control.

Which is exactly what I want to feel. What I need to experience.

"Bite me, *Alpha*," I tell him—the beast. Then I focus on the human side and clarify: "Claim me with your knot."

# GREY

THIS FEMALE IS GOING to be the death of me.

The logical part of me knows we should talk.

But the animal part of me is refusing to adhere to reason. My beast is raging. Because our female just asked me to bite her. To knot her. *To claim her.*

It's our destiny, something my soul knows as well as my mind. Yet there's so much left unsaid between us. So many riddles.

While lost in what she thought was a dream, she confessed that she intends to endure something for me. *Endure what?* I want to demand again, to make her tell me the truth. To confide whatever fate she's witnessed in her mind.

Because whatever that fate is… it's deeply unsettling to her. I could see it in her eyes, hear it in her voice. I want her to explain, to tell me what I don't know.

But she's asking me to do this for her first.

To give her my knot. To give her a moment of us—her words.

Followed by *"It's all I've ever desired. For myself."*

It feels selfish to demand that she satisfy my curiosity first.

My Omega needs me to put her needs above my own.

Which ironically suits my beast's present desires, too.

Claiming her won't be a hardship. It'll be the opposite. It'll be amazing. The most incredible experience of my lifetime.

It feels almost wrong that I will gain as much pleasure, if not more, than my intended mate.

But it's what she wants.

So it's what I'm going to give her.

I don't tell her that with words. I simply kiss her instead.

But it's not just any kiss.

It's a vow.

One I've never given to anyone else. Because she's the first I've ever kissed. It wasn't just my knot that I saved for a future mate; it was the intimacy, too.

Orgasms have always been a clinical exercise for me. A way to escape into temporary bliss and curb the feral urges of my beast.

However, true pleasure comes from the soul. From the mate bond formed between an Alpha and his fated Omega.

I've known that all my life.

Chose not to waste my precious moments on past dalliances and saved the purest parts of myself for my true half.

*For Ashlyn.*

"I'll try to be gentle," I say against her mouth, needing her to know that I want to respect her. Please her. Make this a good experience, not a terrifying one. "My beast may not want to cooperate, but I'll do my best to tame him for you."

"I'm built to handle your aggression, Alpha," Ashlyn replies. "Don't belittle me by holding back."

*Fuck.* Her words make my inner animal roar in approval, causing my knot to pulse painfully in response.

She's going to send me into a rut.

A violent state of *need*.

An uncontrollable desire to *fuck*.

Not just once.

But over and over again, until my beast is satisfied that she's ours.

He wants me to take every part of her—mouth, pussy, and ass.

Mark her with my teeth.

Make her hold my knot inside her sweet cunt for fucking *days* while I feed her my seed and force her to subsist on my essence alone.

It's a dangerous dance.

Yet her fearless gaze tells me she's not afraid to embrace it. "Knot me, Alpha," she demands, her sultry voice making it hard to believe that this woman is basically a virgin. That she's never taken another to her bed.

But I can see the innocence in her gaze and hear it in her gasp when I reach between us to palm her slick heat.

She's never been touched there.

It's clear in the way her nostrils flare, her pupils dilating with a mixture of fear and interest.

"I'm at least going to prepare you," I tell her.

Ashlyn frowns, the expression adorable. "Prepare me?"

I smile and press a kiss to her lips. "Sweet Omega of mine…" I nip her jaw, then lower my mouth to her neck and nibble her raging pulse. "There is much I will teach you."

Because she's not the only one who has dreamt of her intended mate.

My mind may not have formed a comprehensible picture, but I've fantasized about taking an Omega for a very long time. How I would seduce my intended. The ways I wanted to make her scream my name.

"I'm going to introduce you to a whole new manner of existence," I promise her, kissing a path to her breasts. "By the time I'm through with you, all you'll be able to see are stars."

She's about to say something but halts on a breath as I take her nipple between my teeth.

Her pretty eyes meet mine, expectation glinting in their blue depths.

But I don't pierce the skin.

Instead, I roll the little rosebud with my tongue.

Her lashes flutter, and her head falls back on a groan.

I smile and do it again, then suck her peak deep into my mouth while palming her opposite tit.

"Oh, Oracle," she breathes.

"Just Grey," I murmur, taking hold of her wet nipple with my fingers before moving my mouth to her other breast. "*Alpha* will do, too."

Since she's said she's not afraid of my inner beast.

Which means he can officially be set free.

I'm still going to contain him where I can, but if Ashlyn wants to truly experience my virility, then that's what I'm going to give her.

*After I finish preparing her*, I think, my finger sliding through her slick center before finding her tight entrance. Just feeling her clench down around my intrusion tells me this is the right thing to do.

Because my cock is not going to fit inside her in this state.

I release a little rumble, desiring more slick, and my

Omega moans in response, her body writhing as her arousal coats my hand.

"Such a good girl," I growl at her, causing her to squeeze my finger as she releases more of that sweet essence. "Fuck, I need to taste you."

Because the alluring scent of her pussy is all around me now.

She reminds me of spring after a long, harsh winter. The scent of flowers blossoming in the rain. A beckoning of sorts, daring my inner wolf to come out of hibernation and play.

This time, my growl is due to my growing need, which has her whimpering in response. Omegas are slaves to their Alphas' desires, making the reverberations purposeful and sometimes cruel.

But she's not in distress.

She's turned on.

*And very fucking wet.*

I kiss a path down her flat belly to her trimmed mound and lower to the heaven waiting for me between her thighs. "I'm going to lick up every drop," I tell her. "Then make you come so hard on my tongue that you release every ounce of slick that you possess."

Her lips part like she's about to say something, but all that comes out is a scream as I seal my lips over her clit and *suck.*

Unintelligible words leave her mouth on a gasp, the sight of it mesmerizing in its innocence. It's like she's never considered this kind of pleasure before.

And I fucking love that.

Love that I'm going to be her first.

Love that she's never experienced another man between her legs.

Only me. *Only ever me…*

I release another rumble right against her sensitive bud as I thrust a second finger into her and smile as she falls apart beneath me.

The way the orgasm hits her tells me it hadn't fully built, just exploded without warning.

I purr in approval, causing her to shudder in response as her body engages in conflicting needs. She's still coming, yet she's relaxing, too.

But not for long…

I lick her deep, indulging myself in her taste as her limbs shake from the onslaught of euphoria still flooding her veins. "You remind me of a sweet rainfall," I murmur, devouring her with my mouth. "My wolf *loves* the rain."

And now I know why.

It's because of her.

Her pussy.

Her slick.

*Her pleasure.*

I've been primed for her my whole fucking life. Just as she's been for me.

And I'm going to make this union between our souls last for-fucking-ever.

I drag my tongue through her folds from opening to clit, lapping her up like a starved man. I've never tasted such ecstasy. It's decadent. Perfect. *Addictive.*

She's my new meal of choice.

I'll feast between her thighs for eternity if she allows it.

"*Grey*," she groans, her fingers in my hair as she tries to tug me away from her throbbing center. "I…"

"More," I growl, ensuring the reverberation goes through her entire cunt.

She screams in response, her slick channel clamping down around my fingers. I pull them out and let the slick pour out of her, then slide three back inside her and curl them up to her G-spot.

"*Alpha!*" she shrieks, clearly never having experienced that before, then flies into another climax that has her panting in response.

I lick her clean, just like I said I would, then drag my teeth across her swollen nub.

The way she squirms tells me it's sensitive, which I love.

Because I did that to her.

And I've only just begun.

Her grip in my hair turns harsh as I close my lips over her again, but I ignore the pull and instead flick her with my tongue.

"Oh, *Grey*, I don't think... I don't know... *Oh my fates...*"

I place a palm on her belly to hold her down as she tries to scramble off the bed, my other hand still working between her thighs as I suck hard on her abused little nub.

She's crying now.

Begging me to stop.

Demanding I keep going.

And shouting for my knot.

It's beautiful. It's chaotic. *It's a fantasy come to life...*

When she falls apart a third time, I finally release her sweet clit from my mouth and crawl up over her to watch the emotions filter across her features.

She's still coming.

Still squirming.

Still crying.

And I suddenly have the urge to lick up her tears, to have every part of her inside me.

So I do. I trace a path along her cheeks, then settle on her mouth and let her taste herself on my tongue.

She clings to me like she's famished, her nails

embedding in my shoulders as I lie between her splayed thighs.

"*Oh*," she moans when my cock touches her sore nub, the hot flesh throbbing against my shaft.

I rub her, drawing a protest from her lips, but I ignore it and continue saturating my cock with her arousal. "You're going to have to learn how to take more," I tell her. "Because I want to spend days making you come with my tongue against your pussy."

"I don't… Grey, I don't…"

"You can and you will," I promise her, kissing her with a tenderness I don't feel—because all I want to do is fucking ravage her. But for her, I temper the urge for a moment to give her time to heal from my sensual assault. "We're going to spend days together in your nest, where we're going to live on each other's pleasure."

I'll feed her my cock and my seed.

And she'll feed me her sweet pussy.

Her legs tighten around me. "I don't know if I can," she pants, her blue eyes smoldering as she looks up at me. "You just… you just…"

"Devoured you?" I suggest. "Introduced you to what my mouth can do? Treated your pussy like my own personal dessert?"

She shudders. "This… I never knew…" She swallows, then trembles again as I move against her slick folds.

When my head touches her clit, she jolts, the action making me chuckle. "You'll get used to coming for me, Omega," I tell her. "Because now that I've started, I never intend to stop." I reach between us again, this time taking hold of my cock to drag it through her heat once more. "I'm going to knot you now, Ashlyn."

Her eyes widen, her lips parting like she might utter a protest.

But that protest dies when I introduce my head to her entrance.

She digs her nails into me again, her pupils so wide I can barely see the blues of her irises now. I'm staring at her wolf. And she's challenging me to *take*.

I let her animal see my inner beast, too.

And I swear I hear a small whine come from my Omega.

Not a whine of submission, but a whine of *need*.

Ashlyn made it clear that she's dreamt of our fate for a very long time. She stated that she was not only waiting for me, but ready for me.

And I can see the proof of that in her gaze now.

"I'm sorry it took so long for us to find one another," I say.

Then punch my hips against hers and enter her tight cunt in a single thrust.

# ASHLYN

*FATES, I'm on fire...*

Grey just ripped me in half.

He... he put that monster between his legs inside me... and... *Oh my Oracle...*

My back bows off the bed, my body fighting the intense intrusion of an Alpha's *cock.*

I'm pretty sure I screamed.

And now I'm crying.

But he isn't moving. He's holding me close, his purr grounding me in a way that's at odds with the agony splintering up from my core.

I thought I could take him. Told him to unleash his beast. But I... I didn't expect it to... to...

His lips caress mine, the touch momentarily distracting me from the pain. When his tongue enters my mouth, I let him lead and simply fall into his kiss while he continues to purr.

It's then that I realize his palms are roaming gently up and down my sides, providing me with another kind of comfort. A tender one. It's so at odds with his size, so at odds with the sensations echoing below.

But I suddenly feel cherished.

Respected.

Adored.

I feel like I'm *his*.

It's an amazing moment of clarity, a realization that grounds me in the moment and makes me forget everything else. All that matters is this. His touch. His mouth. *His knot...*

Fates, this male is destroying all my expectations. Rewriting every fantasy. Introducing me to a new existence. A craving I never thought was even possible.

All I want is more.

All I desire is him.

All I need is for him to "*Move.*"

He chuckles, and I realize I've voiced that last word out loud. As a command.

Before I can say anything else, he pulls his hips away from mine and slams into me again. "Like that, Omega?" he asks.

I try to respond, I do, but I'm too busy gasping for air. Because *wow*. That's *so much* better than a toy.

When he does it again, I see the stars he mentioned.

And then I lose track of reality.

Because he's kissing me. Touching me. *Fucking me.*

It's amazing. It's terrifying. It's *exhilarating*.

I'm pretty sure he's going to break me, and I don't think I care. I just hold on to his shoulders as he destroys me with his thrusts.

So harsh.

So intense.

*So dominant.*

I feel owned. Claimed. *Utterly consumed*.

Yet safe at the same time.

Because I know he won't truly hurt me. Maybe a little with his teeth or his incredible strength, but it'll never be intentional.

*He's my mate.*

Well, not quite.

Still just fated.

*But, oh my Oracle, I can't breathe…*

Every part of me is overheated from his movements, and I've lost myself to his kiss. His tongue. His *taste*.

Or my taste, I guess.

Arousal.

So much fire.

*Fates…*

I wrap my legs around him and squeeze, holding on as he drills me into the mattress. His beast stares down at me now, his animal having taken full control, and all I can do is accept his impending claim.

My wolf snarls inside, the sound ferocious in nature, yet it's a response to the Alpha looking at us through Grey's gaze.

She wants to *mate*.

She's daring him to claim.

And the way he's looking at us says he fully accepts that challenge.

I've never seen this moment, never experienced the euphoria of a mating bite. Not even in my wildest dreams did I think this would ever happen.

From the kissing to the orgasms to the knotting… I never foresaw any of it. And I'm glad for that. Glad that I get to experience it for the first time—*with Grey*.

He palms my cheek, his forehead falling to mine as he

slows his pace. "Fuck, Ashlyn," he breathes. "I can feel my knot getting ready to explode, and it's… it's fucking intense."

I thread my fingers through his thick hair, loving the soft texture. "I can't wait to feel your knot, Alpha."

"I can't wait to feel it either, Omega," he whispers, and there's something raw in his voice. Something left unsaid.

I wonder what it is.

But in the next moment, he's rutting into me, and his beast is back in his gaze, staring down at me with a hunger that touches my very soul.

I try to move my head to the side, to expose my neck for him, but his palm on my cheek holds me steady. He's looking at me like he intends to possess me. And he's forcing me to witness his need. His imminent claim. *His devotion.*

This is all so unexpected in the best way.

I never thought Grey would want this—want *us.*

*Because I've relied solely on my visions,* I think dizzily. *They're nothing compared to this reality.*

A reality where Grey is kissing me again. His palms are on my hips now, holding me in place as he ruts into me.

Then his hand sneaks between us, something I don't understand until his thumb strokes my clit.

I squeeze my legs and other parts around him, the sensation too much. Yet it's not enough at the same time. I'm overwhelmed. I'm panting. I'm *screaming* as he does it again and again.

"*Grey!*"

"You're going to come around my cock," he growls, his lips at my ear now. "Only then will I give you my knot, Omega."

Every part of me positively *burns.*

I think I forget how to breathe. How to think. How to *exist*.

Because I'm suddenly soaring. Lost in the stars. Blinking into the darkness. Quivering and shaking from the onslaught of passion.

It's a euphoric episode like no other.

More incredible than anything—

A shriek escapes me as the sensation *doubles* from an unexpected pressure in my lower abdomen.

Wait, no… not unexpected.

*Grey's knot.*

He's coming.

He's roaring.

He's *vibrating*.

I shake beneath him, lost to our joining. Consumed by our pleasure. *Overcome* by—

A sharp pain echoes from my neck, Grey's teeth sinking into my skin and *claiming* me as his.

Just like he said he would.

Only it's far more vicious than I could ever have visualized. Because his beast is the one leaving his mark. I'm not sure if Grey partially shifted his jaw or if his human teeth are just that sharp, but his bite is impactful. It stings.

But then… then it feels good. Warm. *Right.*

His tongue swipes at the wound, his eyes holding mine as our bodies continue to convulse in the throes of ecstasy.

Then it renews again as the bond snaps into place.

Z-Clan Alphas claim with a single bite.

It's different from V-Clan wolves that require reciprocation.

I don't have to do anything at all, just exist and find my fated mate.

Which I've done.

And now he's finished it, our spirits combining in a plane of existence that neither of us will ever truly touch or see.

But we can feel it. Sense our heartbeats joining as one. Revel in the eternal dance between our souls.

His lips find mine, kissing the life out of me as our bodies writhe in passion, the pleasure unending. It's almost to the point of discomfort, yet not.

Because all I desire is more.

More caresses.

More tongue.

More *knotting*.

Which is insane, as his knot is still inside me, clinging to my inner wall and forcing me to join him in this matrimonial moment.

I'm not in heat yet, but I can sense it coming now, like this beast has awakened my estrus.

Maybe he has.

I'm not sure I care.

I simply never want this moment to end.

"I'm okay with your plan to pleasure me in the nest," I tell Grey.

He smiles against my lips. "Then you're already learning." He kisses me softly. "You're incredible, Ashlyn. And this…" He moves his hips against mine. "I think I'll just… live here. For eternity."

I laugh.

Then I overhear an inkling of *why* from his mind.

It's… it's a strand of knowledge that warms the bond forming between us mentally.

A strand of knowledge that has my eyes widening. "You've never knotted anyone before?"

His icy eyes stare down at me as he responds, "No, Ashlyn. I waited for my mate. For *you*."

I blink up at him, astounded. And also… also *touched*.

My vision blurs. "Wow," I breathe, unsure of what else to say or how to express what I'm feeling.

I waited for him because I knew of his existence and being with anyone else felt wrong.

But for him to also wait for me?

I shiver. "I can't believe you haven't knotted an Omega before."

"I've also never kissed anyone before," he says, his nose touching mine. "Only you. And only ever you, too."

My lips part. "I would never have guessed that," I admit, thinking about how well he dominated my mouth.

Granted, I don't have any experience to compare it to.

But I'm rather certain his skill is superior.

He chuckles and kisses me again, his mind sharing all sorts of curious revelations. I can't hear him clearly, just pick up on ribbons of thought.

*Strange.* I expected to be able to hear him clearly. To *talk* to him.

Maybe that part of the connection comes later for Z-Clan wolves? I'm not quite sure. But as his knot begins to subside, I'm suddenly more consumed by the notion of us doing this all over again.

It seems Grey is on the same page because he deepens our kiss and his cock is still hard. When his hands start to roam over me, I know we're going to play again.

And I practically melt into him.

Because yes, *these* are the memories I crave. The memories I *need*.

We may have rewritten the future.

And everything might change from horrific to something unfathomably worse.

But at least I'll know it was worth it.

Because now I'll go to my grave knowing that I truly lived.

That I experienced a mate bond.

That, for a moment in time, I had an Alpha who cared for me properly.

*Thank you, Alpha,* I mentally whisper to him, aware that he can't hear me, but needing to say it anyway. *Thank you.*

# GREY

## Two Days Later

Ashlyn sits at the table, her eyes wide as magic hums in the air.

It seems she was right about adopting some of my magic via our bond. If only the power went both ways. And I'm still trying to determine *why* I can't hear her at all.

She said she can sense some of my thoughts, but it's not always clear.

And neither of us can communicate mentally.

It's… strange.

I watch as she draws a protective rune on herself, just like the one I dismantled an hour ago so she could practice.

Her brow pinches when it doesn't glow properly at the end, and I wait to see if she figures out why.

I sip my coffee—something I made from an old coffee maker I found in the dusty cabinet—and watch her start over again.

She'll ask me if she wants to know what she's missing.

While she busies herself with that, I mentally check all the wards around the property. I put them up when we first arrived—almost immediately after tucking her into a bed beneath a mountain of blankets—and have been mentally recharging them several times a day since.

So far, there haven't been any signs of life anywhere near here.

Yet I still can't seem to shadow Ashlyn out of here. And anytime I try to do so on my own, it feels wrong. Wobbly, even. So I always stop before the shadow takes hold. It's never happened to me before, and the issue is clearly linked to Ashlyn somehow.

I've sent Cael a few messages about it, but he hasn't replied yet. Which is making me question if the watch was damaged somehow during our escape from the cave. Or maybe from all the snow we plowed through to reach this cabin.

"*Ugh*," Ashlyn growls. "What am I doing wrong?"

I glance at her arm. "You're missing a dash. Want me to show you where?" I found out yesterday that she prefers to learn by doing, so I'm trying to respect that process.

"Yes."

I nod and step forward to draw a line for her near the corner. The rune instantly lights up with golden flares, and she basically snarls at it.

I help her remove it and say, "Try again while I call Cael." Because I really don't like that he's been radio silent since I left his office five days ago. I should have called him earlier after he didn't respond to my messages, but Ashlyn distracted me with her *needs*.

*And what sweet needs those were,* I muse, running my gaze over her before stepping outside to bring up Cael's number.

It rings once before flashing an error that reads "No Signal."

I stare at it, then look at the satellite connection. The strength isn't great, but the status is still green. Which means I definitely have a signal.

Frowning, I try again, and the same thing happens.

I bring up my messages to see if they've gone through, and they all have a "Delivered" status.

To test it, I try Dixon's direct line.

And the same thing happens.

"Right." I remove the watch and carry it back inside to where Ashlyn is almost done drawing the rune again. I toss the broken tech onto the counter and watch her concentrate.

But then she stills, her expression going blank.

"Ashlyn?" I prompt after she doesn't move for more than ten seconds. She doesn't even appear to be breathing.

I walk over and wave my hand in front of her face.

Nothing.

*A vision?* I wonder, not sure if I should interrupt or… I don't know.

I can't *hear* anything, which is infuriating. She's supposed to be mine. I bit her. I *claimed* her. *So why can't I fucking—*

Ashlyn comes alive with a gasp, her eyes wide as she looks at me. "*Cael*," she breathes. "Did you… did you talk to Cael?"

My brow furrows. "No. The watch is broken."

She shakes her head. "You have to go to him, Grey. *You need to go*."

"What did you see?" I ask her, needing to understand.

"There isn't time," she tells me, sounding frantic. "Forget about me and *go*."

Is she mad? "Forget—"

"Now!" she demands, her eyes filling with tears. "Please, Grey. Please listen to me."

"Okay," I tell her. "But I'm coming right back."

Her blue irises look glassy from the unshed tears. "Go, Grey."

My gaze narrows. "I will *never* forget you, *mate*," I growl at her, needing that to be said between us. "I'll be right back."

My shadowing ability ignites with ease, which is strange since it was still giving me trouble only an hour ago. But I accept it and take myself to Lunar Sector.

Only Ashlyn's final words—which she must have voiced as I engaged my shadow—seem to chase after me into the darkness. "*Goodbye, Grey.*"

I frown, not liking those words. Particularly as they seem to be echoing through my head with a finality that leaves me feeling unsteady.

*The moment I finish here...*

My thought trails off as my surroundings begin to appear, the rocky wall not at all like the elegant office I was aiming for with my shadowing.

*What the fuck?*

I spin around, noting the large cavern overhead and the abundance of candles.

No views of the former Russian archipelago that Lunar Sector now owns.

No water.

No *ice*.

Just rocks and candles.

I attempt to shadow again, only to find my power nonexistent.

My eyes widen, my fingers automatically attempting to draw a rune. But I seem to possess no magic at all.

*Just like when I was collared by my father.*

Goose bumps erupt down my arms, which I now realize are bare.

Because I shadowed in my fucking sweatpants.

I'm not even wearing shoes.

I was so quick to do what Ashlyn requested, her urgency making me act without thinking it through.

And now...

*Where the fuck am I?*

"Hello, brother," a ghost from my past says, the deep voice unmistakable as it echoes around the cave. "Welcome home."

*Home?* I think, looking around again, my eyes widening. *Kodiak Sector...*

I shadowed to Lunar Sector and somehow ended up in *Kodiak Sector* instead.

Only it's nothing like the images my father showed me as a child.

All the ice. The snow. The igloos.

This is a fucking tunnel system. *A cave with a lot of candles,* I think, recalling what Ashlyn said about my sister.

*"How many candles?"* I asked her.

*"Thousands upon thousands,"* she whispered.

I see them all now, the candles flickering throughout every inch of this cavern, illuminating it from within.

*We must be in a carved-out mountain,* I think. *Fuck.*

"You're wondering how you ended up here, I assume," Spruce says. "Or perhaps wondering how I rose from the dead?"

I clench my jaw, not sure I like where this is heading at all. Particularly as I'm still magically collared somehow. "What am I doing here, *brother*?" I ask him.

"Well, you shadowed here," he explains, his voice taking on a taunting edge. "Though, I don't think this is where you meant to go, is it? Maybe back to Lunar Sector, perhaps?"

Ice drizzles down my spine. "What did you do?" I demand, trying to find him in the cave.

But he appears to be masked in shadows—a bit of irony, considering how I ended up here.

"I didn't do anything. Our sister, however…" He finally steps into the light, his blond hair illuminated by the candles around him.

But it's the glass of liquid that catches my eye more.

It's full of blood.

I can smell it from here.

Blood bolsters a V-Clan wolf's magic, making it a necessary drink for our kind. Though, I find I can go months without it and not feel any different, maybe because of my Z-Clan genetics.

However, my brother never imbibed while growing up. Mostly because our father forbade it, said it was too vampiric and he wasn't going to raise vampires as children.

Interesting that my twin is drinking it now.

Also interesting that I can't sense or feel him at all.

That's why I thought he was dead—our twin-bond severed, and I felt his life disappear.

It seems that was a bad assumption on my part.

"Would you like to see her?" he asks, causing me to arch a brow. "Our sister, I mean. She's quite the attraction around here."

My stomach clenches, my heart suddenly in my throat. *Nikiski is here.*

This is part of the visions that Ashlyn saw—the cave, my sister, the candles.

But not my brother.

*What the fuck is going on?* I want to demand, but I refuse to play into whatever game Spruce is trying to initiate.

Instead, I calmly ask, "Do you want me to see her?" I infuse my words with boredom, the skill one I mastered with Cael as a best friend.

He's the stronger political player in the field.

But there's a reason he assigned me the title of Second-in-Command.

"What I want is my new toy," Spruce says, then takes a drink from his glass, his forest-green eyes—the same as our father's—closing in momentary bliss. "But you left her to the outlaws, I see."

My calm mask nearly slips.

Because I really don't like what he's saying or what I think he's implying.

"Which is fine, I guess," he goes on. "They'll break her in for me. Make it easier to tame her once she's mine."

*Ashlyn,* I think. *No. He can't be talking about her. How would he even know about her?*

"Nikiski has struggled with that little brat for eons," he continues. "Having to implant images, then change things around once thwarted." He swirls his drink, then takes another sip. "The pretty seer has been so fucking elusive. I honestly can't wait to choke her with my knot down her throat, make her pay for all the effort."

I swallow, my beast growling inside.

I don't understand what he means about implanting images, but *pretty seer* sounds too much like Ashlyn. *My little riddler.*

"Anyway," he says, taking a step back. "If you'll come with me, I'll show you to Nikiski. Let you say hi for old times' sake. Just know that she can't say much back."

My heart skips a beat. I want to ask what he means. I want to ask how he forced me to shadow here. I want to ask how he's disconnected his soul from our twin-bond. I want to ask what really happened to our sister that night.

Because everything I've researched, everything I thought I knew, is clearly wrong.

Nikiski isn't in the Omega slave trade at all. She's *here*. In this cavern. In Kodiak Sector.

*Fuck.*

He's waiting for me to walk with him, so I slide my hands into my pockets and feign a confidence I don't feel.

I have no weapons.

Barely any clothes.

And my powers have been thwarted by some magical barrier that I can't see.

What I do have is my mind. My fists. *And motivation.*

But I can't exactly use any of those items until I know what I'm up against.

So I do the only thing I can do—I obey my brother's request and follow him… *into hell.*

# ASHLYN

## Nomad Lands, Canada

*Grey's gone.*

I felt it when he left, the finality of the moment. It was too much like my visions. Yet it was starkly different as well.

Nothing is what it seems.

Everything is murky.

And my mind still isn't clear.

Which is infuriating. I can't see *anything*. It's like I'm lost in an abyss. But something happened in Lunar Sector. Something *catastrophic*.

I…

All I could see was *blood*.

*And Cael's head… rolling…*

I grab my hair and tug, hating that I don't know what happened. Whether or not it was stopped. *If Grey is okay…*

The moment he shadowed, I felt our tentative link *snap*.

I'm not sure how it happened, but it's like we're no longer mated.

*He bit me.*

*He claimed me.*

*He* bonded *me.*

So why can't I feel him anymore?

*What's happening in Lunar Sector?*

I pace the room, my heart racing in my chest.

It's been *hours* since Grey left. *Hours* since I said goodbye to him.

*"I'll be right back"* were his final words. And that triggered something in me. A vision. But it left before it could properly form, leaving me blinking in confusion.

*Something is very wrong.* But I can't identify what I'm feeling or why.

"This is maddening," I mutter out loud, still pacing. "Utter insanity." I've never been this blind before. Never been this lost or unable to—

A howl pierces the air, the sound of it sending goose bumps scattering up and down my arms.

That's a sound I know well.

And not just because it's an Alpha announcing his intent.

It's a specific sound from my nightmares of the future.

A nightmare... that's unveiling now.

I shake my head. *But I'm not in heat.*

In my dreams, I was always in heat.

It was always dark.

*And I was always in that lair...*

Nothing about this cabin. Nothing about Grey knotting me. Nothing about his *bite.*

I spin around, my mind racing with confusion, my heart pounding in my chest.

I'm panicking.

I... I know I'm panicking.

*I need it to stop,* I think, dizzy. *I need to breathe!*

Oracle, I've lost complete control. I just… I just need to…

I close my eyes and force myself to inhale. *Focus, Ash*, I tell myself. *Focus.*

There are defensive wards all around this cabin. I felt Grey bolstering them earlier while I was—

My eyes flash open, and I look down at my arm. "The rune…" I never finished it. I've been too busy worrying about Lunar Sector and Grey to complete my task.

*Foolish*, I tell myself, shaking my head.

Then I concentrate on reigniting the protective mark.

I was so close before, just missed a single dash.

"You can do this," I whisper. "You *have* to do this."

I wanted to learn these runes for a reason. And tonight might very well be that reason.

My finger shakes as I draw the magic across my skin.

"Come on," I coach myself, pausing to take another deep breath.

Which is when that howl pierces the air, closer now.

*Too close.*

*Why are the wards not firing?* I wonder, glancing out the window at the setting sun.

"Don't," I chastise myself. "Rune first."

Inhaling once more, I breathe out through my mouth and *focus*.

*Dash. Cross. Point. Upward. Circle around. Pause. Another dash. Crisscross. Point.* I consider the symbol, aware that I'm missing a few details. It's tedious, and the order in which I execute each part of it is important. *But I think… Yes!*

The rune lights up in gold, sending a rush of sensation over my skin.

*Oh, that's new*, I think, shivering a little from the static electricity rolling through me. *Why didn't I feel that when Grey did it?*

"Does that mean I did it wrong?" I mutter to myself. "Should I—"

A sharp pang hits my abdomen, causing me to double over on a wheeze of pain.

*Ow. Ow. Ow.*

*What…?*

*I don't…*

My knees hit the ground, my body starting to convulse as waves of agony sweep over me.

*The rune,* I think, looking down at my arm. But I can't seem to move… enough… to… *Oracle!*

It takes everything in me to try to breathe through the churning in my abdomen.

*My estrus,* I realize. *I'm going into heat…*

But this sudden…

I begin to shake.

And instantly I'm cascaded into darkness, locked in that cavern, the one holding Grey's sister.

I've never known how I recognized her. She looks nothing like her brother with her long, dark hair and equally dark eyes. But I *know* her as I look at her.

And she knows me.

There's a hint of desperation in her gaze that's always there, one I've never truly considered until now.

Because my visions don't usually stare back at me.

However, she's definitely looking at me right now, her expression pleading with me to…

*To what?* I wonder.

She's locked in a cage, her mouth bound by a gag.

But her eyes convey meaning. Her eyes *see* me.

I stare back, taking in the scene all around her.

Her cage is made of glass. She's naked. Utterly exposed. But that doesn't seem to be the cause of her current expression.

There's anger in her dark eyes.

No, not just anger... *fury.*

This female is *raging* inside.

There are Alphas all around her, watching her every move. But she ignores them. Ignores the jeers. Ignores the cord attached to her arm...

*What?* I've never seen that before.

It's not a cord, though.

It's... it's like an IV.

And it's draining her blood into something.

My brow furrows as I watch one of the Alphas—a male who kind of reminds me of Grey—walk up to fill his glass from a spout.

*Oh, fates...*

They're draining Grey's sister.

*But why?*

I look at her again, and she glares back like she's annoyed.

*Are you trying to communicate with me?* I wonder, utterly confused by this vision. Because it doesn't feel vision-like so much as *real.*

I start to shake my head, trying to clear it, but as I do, I catch sight of Grey.

*Grey.*

My lips part. "*Grey!*"

He's unconscious by the glass, a bullet hole in his head.

He can't die.

He's... he's immortal.

But... but he looks very dead.

*What happened? Has this happened? Will this happen? I don't...*

Nikiski raises her hands, drawing me back to her, and holds up seven fingers before tapping her wrist.

She's still staring straight at me as her hand turns into

an O shape. I frown as she touches her cheek and then her ear.

*I don't understand.*

She does it again.

*Seven.*

*Wrist.*

*O shape from cheek to ear.*

Then everything goes dark, and I wake up on the floor of the cabin, looking at the ceiling above.

That symbol clearly means something, along with the number seven.

*Seven o'clock?* I wonder. *Seven hours?*

And what does the other...?

My stomach churns again, reminding me of my approaching heat just as that howl echoes outside once more.

It's getting closer.

*They* are getting closer.

Visions of savage Alphas filter through my thoughts, these being fresh images, not ones from my past.

Because my future has been rewritten.

I'm on a new path now.

A worse one.

Because those Alphas are destined to rape me in the same bed I shared with Grey.

I palm my belly, tears pricking my eyes.

His sister was trying to tell me something. Which is impossible. I don't communicate with victims via visions; I simply *see* them.

*Yet she saw me,* I think, considering the vision. *Is she a seer, too?*

She's part V-Clan, part Z-Clan Omega.

It's... it's very possible.

Which means... which means she can see the future. Or perhaps has another ability tied to fortune-telling.

*Wait...*

I look down at my rune and see it glowing defensively on my skin. I thought that just meant it was working, that it was glowing to signify that it was on.

But what if it's more than that?

What if it's *actively* protecting me?

I thought dragons might be the source messing with my visions. I never considered that it could be another Z-Clan Omega.

*Nikiski.*

*Has she been feeding me images?* I sit up off the ground, ignoring the pang in my stomach. *Lunar Sector...*

Was it all a lie? Cael's death? The blood?

I can't see any of it now.

It's like the vision never existed.

I look down at the rune again.

*And it happened when I wasn't protected...*

"Oracle," I breathe.

That explains all the fuzziness, the shifting visions, the *confusion.*

I have no idea what was real and what was implanted.

But I can *see* the Alphas coming for me now.

Just as I can *see* Grey on the floor with a bullet wound in his head. He's even wearing the same sweats he left in.

However, there's a lot of blood on him. Open wounds. *Lashes*, I recognize. *He's being tortured.*

Now or in the future?

That part I can't determine.

But he's alive.

I can feel him now that the rune is in place. I can feel his wards firing, too.

It's like everything has suddenly become clear again.

If only I could *hear* him.

*Grey!* I shout, wishing our connection worked. *Grey, if you can hear me, tell me how to find you!*

Nothing.

I growl. *I am not giving up. There has to be a way...*

I push up off the floor, forcing myself to move through the pain and walk over to the windows and doors. I need to do something to protect myself while I puzzle through these pieces.

I have to find Grey.

Help him save Nikiski.

*Anything* to—

A buzzing sound has me freezing in place.

Then I slowly turn to see Grey's watch lighting up on the counter.

My lips part. I didn't even realize he'd left it there.

The screen goes dark in the next moment, though.

*Ashlyn,* I hear Grey, his voice in my head the most amazing sound ever to exist.

*Grey!*

*Ashlyn...*

*I'm here!* I tell him.

*Watch,* he says, making me frown.

*What?*

But he's still talking, his words garbled like he's on a phone with a bad signal.

*Don't,* he says.

*Don't what?* I ask, confused.

*Kodiak...*

My heart skips a beat. *Kodiak Sector.*

*Caves,* he thinks next. *But... watch... stand?*

I try to follow what he's saying, but my mind is already thinking through *Kodiak Sector* and *caves.*

Kodiak Sector is a mountainous island.

Is it possible they carved out the insides of a mountain to make a cave? One lit by thousands of candles?

I go grab his watch just as the screen lights up with an incoming call. *Cael.*

I touch the *Pick Up* button, and his face appears. "Ashlyn," he says, appearing relieved. "Where the fuck are you?"

"I don't know," I admit. "Somewhere in Canada, or what used to be Canada?" I shake my head. "But that doesn't matter. Grey is in trouble. He's been taken to a cavern... I... I think it might be in Kodiak Sector. I can't understand him well in my head."

"Kodiak Sector?" he repeats.

"He was trying to shadow to Lunar Sector because I saw something... only I didn't actually see it. I think his sister is messing with my head. Which, actually, do you know what this means?" I replicate the motion Nikiski did in my weird vision of her.

Cael frowns. "No, but it looks like sign language."

"She also kept showing me the number seven and tapping her wrist."

"She?"

"Nikiski," I explain. "She's..." I trail off as a particularly painful spasm rips through my belly. I press my palm to it, trying to quell the ache. Then I bite my lip to keep from moaning out loud.

"Ashlyn?" he asks, sounding concerned.

"Home," someone else says in the background.

"What?" Cael asks.

"That sign means *home*," the deep voice tells him.

I don't know who it is, and I don't care.

Because that makes sense. "She was trying to tell me they're in Kodiak Sector," I manage to force out.

"Are you okay, Ashlyn?" Cael demands.

"I'm fine," I tell him. "It's Grey—I saw him… I *see* him getting shot. You need to help him, Cael. They've done something to him. I… I don't know what. But he was shadowing to Lunar Sector and somehow ended up there. And his sister… she's been manipulating my visions. Though, I don't think she *wanted* to do it."

So it's not a Sylvia situation, like with Prince Tadhg when he'd basically groomed her to do his bidding.

This felt very *forced*, like Nikiski has been fighting whoever has her in custody.

*The man with the glass… the one who looked like Grey.* "Spruce," I realize out loud, another piece of the puzzle clicking into place. "Cael, I think Spruce is alive. Grey's brother. He has Nikiski… and Grey."

I just don't understand what the endgame is.

I can't *see* it.

All I see are those Alphas coming to rip me apart.

"You have to help him, Cael. Promise me you'll help him."

He says something in response, but I can't hear him over the roaring in my ears.

*Oh, fates…* The vision has worsened.

I've accidentally set off a trigger of some kind. I just don't understand what or how, only that the outcome is starting to reveal itself in my mind.

And it's not pleasant.

It's bloody.

Horrific.

*Filled with pain…*

I focus on the window… on the night sky… *It's happening.*

*Tonight is when everything ends.*

"Help him, Cael," I say again. "Save him and Nikiski, and tell him I'll be waiting."

I won't be.

But that's beside the point.

I need Cael to concentrate on Grey. To help Grey. Not me.

I end the call and force myself to focus.

I learned those runes for a reason.

This might be my final night of existence, but I am not going down without a fight.

*Time to prepare for battle...*

# GREY

I can't believe what I'm seeing.

Nikiski is in a fucking *box*.

Naked and gagged.

And her arm is attached to an IV that's draining her blood for Spruce to imbibe.

"What the fuck is this?" I demand, no longer capable of masking my emotions. "Why are you doing this?"

"Power," Spruce says simply. "Specifically, hers. But the only way to control her is to drink."

Nikiski makes a murderous face that tells me she's very much *aware* of her situation. Not only that, but she's very much *alive*.

How many other Omegas would have broken under these conditions?

But not Nikiski.

She's livid. And she ensures Spruce knows that as she glowers at him.

She was spirited growing up, too, often trying to challenge our father's authority. No matter how many times he struck her, she got right back up. Sometimes, it took more effort than others. But she never let him keep her down.

And it seems that spirit has only been emboldened.

I want to feel relieved by that. But I'm too fucking furious to feel much of anything other than anger.

"What are you making her do?" I ask Spruce.

He smiles, his teeth red from her blood. "She's helping me ensnare a powerful seer by implanting visions and confusing fate. And now she's going to help me again, aren't you, darling sister?"

Nikiski narrows her gaze, then freezes as my brother does something with his mind. Something that has our sister collapsing to her knees in a fit of obvious suffering.

I growl, unable to mask the sound, and charge forward.

Only to find my feet *glued* to the ground.

"I'll be with you in a moment," Spruce says casually, his dark eyes on Nikiski as she begins to scream in agony.

Several growls follow the sound, this time from other Alphas as they enter the room.

Except their growls are not ones of fury, but of *hunger*.

They're looking at Nikiski like they want to fucking rip her apart.

"Not yet," Spruce tells them. "*After* the task is done."

My stomach twists with what he means by that. I can only imagine what they'll be allowed to do *after* whatever the fuck this is.

"Hmm, that's frustrating," Spruce murmurs to himself. "I wonder where she learned to do that?"

Nikiski gasps as he seems to release his mental hold on her, his eyes going to me.

"You taught my seer how to protect herself with a rune of some kind. What is it?"

I arch a brow. "*Your* seer?"

"Don't be a fool, brother. You're outnumbered and very much outmatched. Tell me what I need to know, and I'll consider letting you live a useful life somewhere in the cave."

A few of the Alphas grunt.

But Spruce just holds my gaze, his expression utterly unreadable.

I've never been close to my twin, his preference to appease our father growing up varying from my desire to challenge him.

However, it seems the twin I once knew is nothing like the Alpha standing before me.

He's powerful. I can sense it in his aura, feel it radiating all around this cavern.

There is no true hierarchy in Kodiak Sector, just packs that choose to follow a single leader. Very different from Lunar Sector, where Cael is the reigning prince of the entire island.

Although, it appears that my brother is the Alpha of this particular pack. And based on the scents I'm picking up, there are numerous members of this unit.

"Grey," Spruce stresses. "This would be easier if you told me what you did to my little toy."

I fold my arms over my chest. "What happens if I don't?"

He smiles. "Then I'll let them play with you before they play with Nikiski." He gestures to the Alphas approaching. "They adore violent foreplay."

My jaw clenches. "Are you going to keep me handicapped or let me *play* my way?"

He grunts. "You'll be free to use your wolf, if you so choose. Nothing else."

"What a fantastic family reunion," I deadpan.

He scoffs at that. "We haven't been a *family* since the night you betrayed our father, Grey." He faces me fully, his green eyes showcasing a sane yet very angry Alpha male. "What were you going to let them do to me that night, *brother*?"

I don't answer.

Because I was absolutely going to let them do whatever it took to ensure our mother's and sister's safety.

And that included killing Spruce if he got in the way.

Which he did. Only, he fucking shadowed before anyone could stop him.

He smiles again, but it's cold. "I'll be sure to repay you the same favor, then."

I don't comment. Because there's really nothing to say.

"Tell me where I can find my seer," he tries again. "And tell me what you taught her."

I remain silent.

There is nothing he can do to make me give up Ashlyn's location.

He arches a brow, almost like he heard that conviction. Or maybe he sees it in my expression. "I see," he murmurs. "Then I suppose we get to do this the fun way."

Nikiski screams, causing all the hairs along my arms to stand on end.

I look in her direction, confused to see her on all fours, shrieking like she's being assaulted somehow. Yet there's no one nearby.

"I'm letting our sister see what I'm going to allow those Alphas do to her after my new toy arrives," Spruce says conversationally. "Sounds like she's going to enjoy it."

I again try to move but find myself still collared somehow. *Fuck!* When I figure out how to undo whatever magic this is, I'm going to *rip* Spruce apart.

"Not as much as my seer is going to enjoy the gift coming for her, of course," he goes on, his words sending ice through my veins. "We just need to pinpoint her location…" He glances down at his watch, the gesture giving me pause.

Because I left my watch on the counter after it didn't work properly.

"Temporarily release the signal blocker for the whole region," he says, talking to someone through his device. "Then track all incoming and outgoing calls."

My heart stops.

Fuck.

*Fuck.*

*Fuck!*

*Ashlyn!* I shout for her, hoping like hell she can hear me somehow.

She doesn't reply.

So I try again. *Ashlyn!*

Nothing.

*Fuck.*

I… I have to try… I'll just…

*Ashlyn… Don't touch the watch. Do you hear me? Do not touch the watch. They're tracking it in Kodiak Sector, which is where I am. That's where the caves are from your visions. But never mind that. Just don't touch the watch, understand?*

I repeat the words over and over until I hear my brother chuckle, the sound making everything inside me freeze. "Excellent," he says.

I have no idea how much time has passed, as I've been too busy repeating the words to Ashlyn.

Words she obviously never heard.

Because in the next moment, I hear a statement that will forever haunt my nightmares.

"Send up a signal flare in the area to alert all the Alphas nearby that an Omega has gone into heat. And send out the coordinates." His dark gaze finds me as he adds, "Didn't need your help after all, *brother*."

# ASHLYN

## NOMAD LANDS, CANADA

HEAT BLASTS THROUGH MY VEINS, making every motion feel impossible as I try to craft as many wards as possible throughout the house.

There's a basement—which I considered hiding in, but then I'll be trapped when the Alphas make it through the security measures.

And that just seems pointless.

I may as well be upstairs, like my visions suggested, so that I can at least try to jump out of a window. Or watch the sun. Or just... *be a little comfortable while they...*

I swallow, not wanting to finish that train of thought.

Instead, I busy myself with the protective runes.

Which hurts.

*A lot.*

Because it requires standing.

*Come on, Ash...*

The howls are getting louder. Explosions erupt as

Grey's wards are crossed. And I know the Alphas are nearing the cabin.

It's only a matter of maybe an hour now. Probably less.

My stomach churns.

Escaping on the snowmobile isn't an option; I can't operate it in this condition.

I'm about to lose my mind to lust.

*And my body to… a series of ruts.*

I bite my lip to keep from crying. Tears won't help.

All I can do now is try to fight.

I grab Grey's bag of guns and ammunition and drag it upstairs with me. For as long as I'm awake—or as long as I have a working weapon—I'll shoot.

Because I'm going to make these assholes *bleed*.

*You want me?* I think, cocking a shotgun. *Come and fucking get me.*

# GREY

## Kodiak Sector

AGONY SHREDS me from the inside out.

Not because of whatever my brother's "friends" are doing to me, but because of what I *feel* from Ashlyn.

She's terrified.

And she's going into heat.

I can sense her estrus from here, her inner wolf howling for mine.

But I'm fucking tied to a chair and getting the shit beaten out of me.

Because, apparently, when my brother said I could use my wolf, he meant I could attempt to shift like this to fight back.

I haven't bothered.

There's no fucking point.

I take the hits. The kicks. All of it without so much as snarling.

I'm too focused on my mate. On our connection. On her pain.

*Ashlyn,* I whisper, wishing I could shadow to her. *I'm so fucking sorry...*

I should never have left her. I knew something wasn't right. But she insisted, and I... I failed her.

Just like I failed Nikiski all those years ago. Just like I'm failing her now, too.

I hear her weeping in her cage, aware of whatever sadistic plans our brother has in store for her. Or maybe she's crying for me.

I really don't know.

It's been ages since I last saw her. I barely even recognize the woman she's become.

Something cracks—a blow to my jaw—causing me to open my eyes for a moment to see a particularly large Z-Clan Alpha treating my face like his personal punching bag.

I spit out a mouthful of blood.

Then go back to feigning sleep.

It hurts. But nothing compares to what I feel inside.

So many pieces are falling into place.

That rune I put on Ashlyn's arm... that's why I couldn't shadow her. It was protecting her by ensuring she didn't end up in this cave.

I haven't figured out yet *how* my brother tapped into my gifts, but I suspect it has something to do with our twin-bond.

*Which also might be why I'm struggling to fully connect to Ashlyn,* I realize. *He's done something to me.*

But that means I might be able to undo it.

Or use it against him.

Only, I suspect he's been in my head for a long time. Which explains how he not only convinced me he was dead but also persuaded me not to hunt for his body as proof.

*Fuck.*

I have no idea when my brother became this clever. Maybe he always was and I missed it as a child, too caught up in my frustrations with our father.

*Or maybe he's had a mentor,* I think, wondering if he's part of the infamous shadow organization.

Regardless, I need to find a way out of this. A way to return to—

A particularly hard blow to my head knocks me and my chair to the ground.

And all I hear is my brother's laugh.

Except it's not only a sound in my ears.

I hear it… in my mind, too.

*That echo,* I think. *Like how Ashlyn's goodbye echoed. How Spruce's voice seemed to echo when he first started speaking.*

Could that be a potential way in?

I ignore the Alphas as they turn my chair right side up, and focus all of my strength inward. I have to do something. I can't just fucking sit here while my *mate* goes into heat in the middle of a locally organized rutting party.

Because that's basically what my brother has done.

*I'm going to fucking kill him.*

But first, I have to beat him.

*How?* I wonder, searching through my mental space, looking for where my bond to Ashlyn should be. It's there. I feel it—and the terror rippling through it—but I can't seem to follow the line into her mind. It's… it's nonexistent.

*No, that's not right. There's a cloud…*

I frown inside.

*Why is there a cloud?* I try to push it away, but it feels elastic in my mind. *Permanent.*

Which makes no sense.

There shouldn't be anything else there except for Ashlyn.

But rather than try to dismantle it, I go into it and find myself staring at an electric storm of activity. It's like a mental minefield.

In my fucking head.

I narrow my gaze inwardly and slowly navigate through the chaos. *There has to be a way to dismantle this…*

However, before I do that, I look to see where it's rooted and how deep it goes.

*Can I be of some assistance?* a silky voice asks in my head, one I was *not* anticipating hearing today.

*Cillian?*

*Hello, Grey. The cavalry is here.*

It takes all of my strength not to react outward to that statement.

*But it seems you have a bit of a problem that needs to be addressed first,* he murmurs. *Would you like some help?*

Any other day, I would have told the telepath to fuck off.

But today is not that day.

*Yes,* I answer flatly. *I would, actually.*

*Then give me a moment,* Cillian says. *This gift I've inherited from Ivana is still quite new…*

I sit and wait, then nearly sigh in relief as warmth floods my veins. Warmth and *power…*

Somewhere, an Alpha growls.

I sense that it's my brother.

But before he can reach me, I shadow out of the chair to the other side of the room.

At least I know *how* he controlled my shadowing now. It had something to do with the link he bastardized.

A link I now feel again.

His life pulses through me, our twin-bond very much alive.

But it won't be for long.

I shake out my arms and legs, then shadow again when I feel my brother trying to latch back onto my mind. It seems he perfected our father's collaring ability.

*Can you help us pinpoint your location in Kodiak Sector, please?* Cillian asks calmly. *The number seven from your sister isn't helping.*

*The number seven?* I repeat, not following.

*Seven o'clock, I believe,* he replies.

I'm about to ask what he's talking about when a fist to the jaw sends me flying across the room. My brother is on me in an instant, a flash of metal in his hand.

I growl and return the punch with one of my own, then shadow out from beneath him—but not before grabbing the metal from his hand.

I crush it in my palm, my Z-Clan strength finally useful for something.

*Ashlyn was on the shore,* I think at Cillian, panting from exertion as I try to fend off my brother while considering what seven o'clock might mean.

With Nikiski being linked to Ashlyn through visions, perhaps she knows this.

*The only thing I can think of is to go to that location and look for a mountain at your seven o'clock. Because we're inside one of them here in Kodiak Sector.*

*Yes, we've gathered the mountain cave bit, but there are a lot of mountains here.*

*I know,* I mutter, shadowing again to avoid being hit by another Alpha's fist.

There are dozens of them spilling into the room, my brother seeming to have set off some sort of alarm.

He smiles, the look of victory crossing his features.

But it's a look that doesn't last long as I let my beast peek out through my eyes.

I very rarely engage my inner rage.

Though, I've done it once already in the last month.

And I'm about to do it again.

I crack my neck, my arms loose at my sides. Then I give in to the urge to *kill*.

Spruce's lips part as I rip the head off of a nearby Alpha, tossing it to the floor without so much as flinching.

Because this is me at my strongest.

This is me when I'm pissed.

This is me embracing all the fury of my childhood. A fury our father taught me how to foster and grow. A fury I'm about to unleash on all these assholes now.

But specifically, my *twin*.

He growls.

And I growl back.

Then I charge him without giving two shits about all of his friends.

This is between me and my brother.

A man I should have hunted and killed ages ago.

But he tainted my mind.

I'm about to return the fucking favor.

I hit him with a bolt of power from my palm—the bolt infused by a rune I created in my mind.

Because I don't have to draw them. I *am* the creator of wards. They exist inside me. I think of them and they appear. And they do whatever the fuck I want them to do.

Like cast a web through my brother's psyche, give him a dose of his own foggy chaos.

He coughs, then grabs his throat, trying to breathe.

I don't let him. I tell the web to grow and expand and take over his mental space. Make him feel *collared* and *under my control*.

He tries to hit me back via the link Cillian disabled—I feel it ringing in my head. But I swat it away, grateful to be *free*.

But then I hear a shriek from Ashlyn that nearly sends me to my knees.

Our connection *throbs*.

Her terror echoing through me and forcing me to relinquish my control of Spruce.

And then he's on me again, slamming his fist into my jaw, and Ashlyn's cry disappears.

*Fuck.*

It wasn't real.

He manufactured it somehow.

But it sounded so—

Another hit to my face breaks my nose.

A hand collars my throat, metal kissing my skin, and I shadow once more, barely escaping my brother's trick.

I craft a rune and throw it right at his heart before he even realizes I've materialized, then I throw another at his head, his throat, his fucking groin.

All of them send him to the ground in a fit of shocks that have him vibrating on the floor.

I'm done with whatever this is between us. A game. A brotherly bond. I don't fucking care. That *shriek* is the last one he will ever put in my head.

I take two Alphas down on my way to reach him, both of their necks snapping with a pair of violent twists—one in each hand—as I give in to my *rage*. It's a violent side of me that I rarely allow the world to see. But Spruce has earned my wrath.

I throw more runes his way, ensuring he fucking stays down. Then I look for something sharp.

All I see is the glass cage holding our sister, though.

I run for it, not even caring that the thing is going to

fucking shatter, and jump up to slam my body through the glass.

Nikiski must have seen me coming in a vision because she's already flat on the ground, my body sailing over hers as shards spray all over the damn place. I land over her, taking the brunt of the damage. Then grab a particularly jagged piece from the base and yank it out with my bare hand.

It burns against my palm.

Cutting into my skin.

But I don't fucking care.

I walk over and drive the sharp end right into my brother's neck. And then I stab him again. And again. All while he screams into my head.

I can barely hear him over the memory of Ashlyn's shriek.

All I see is *red*.

Blood.

Violence.

*Rage. Rage. Rage.*

The link inside me dies the moment the lights go out in Spruce's eyes, yet I don't stop cutting and stabbing until the last strand is severed.

He needs to *burn*.

But a cry from Nikiski has me spinning toward her as a horde of Alphas approach with salivating expressions.

*She can't stay here,* I think.

*On it,* Cillian replies, reminding me that he's here somewhere. But not in the cavern.

However, magic shimmers in the next moment as Cillian, Kieran, Cael, and Lorcan appear together in all black, weapons drawn.

Nikiski jumps into Cael's side, clinging to him like she

knows him, just as he opens fire on the three Alphas who were approaching her.

Then Cillian turns and throws me something that I catch in midair.

*A miniature fire grenade.*

I almost laugh, but instead I kneel and pull the pin, then stuff the small item into Spruce's mouth. Picking up his body, I toss it over his head and walk away as the thing explodes behind me.

The stench of burning skin follows, my brother's life fully extinguished.

I glance back, just to make sure he's truly on fire, and feel nothing other than fury as I watch his corpse disintegrate.

However, I'm not mad at him. I'm mad at myself. Because I should have known he was alive. Sure, he fucked with my head. But I didn't even feel it.

That backdoor fog, though, explains how he knew about Ashlyn.

And also why he apparently chose to target her.

Though, it doesn't explain how he came to be in charge of this group of Alphas or what exactly happened between him and Nikiski.

She glances back at me, her dark eyes wide. Probably because I'm covered in blood and still in feral mode. That's not going to end anytime soon.

"Grey," she whispers.

"Niki," I return, using the nickname I gifted her as a child.

She runs toward me and throws herself into my arms, not seeming to care at all about the blood.

"I'm so sorry, baby girl," I tell her, using another nickname from our childhood. "I've been trying to find you since that night…"

"I know," she whispers. "I've seen your efforts, big brother." She clings to me, her head buried in my neck. "Thank you, Grey. You're the one who kept me sane. You and Cael, I mean."

"You saw him, too?" I ask, meeting my best friend's gaze over her head. He's standing next to three dead Alphas.

Kieran, Lorcan, and Cillian appear to be taking on the rest.

They won't be able to stay here long before more Z-Clan packs show up.

But I doubt any of those Alphas will have the ability to collar us the way my brother did to me.

"Every night," Nikiski whispers, making me frown.

Then I remember what I asked—if she saw Cael, too.

"Oh," I reply.

"You need to go," Nikiski says, pushing away from me. "You need to go *now*."

Those words are similar to what was said to me mere hours ago.

Which has my heart stalling in my chest. "*Ashlyn…*"

"I'll see you in Lunar Sector," Nikiski promises. "Thank you, but *go*."

For a beat, I'm torn. I've spent a century trying to find my little sister and fully expected her to need my comfort to heal.

But she's telling me to go after my mate.

*My mate who is in very real danger…*

I hold my sister's gaze for another beat.

Then shadow into the midst of chaos.

There's blood everywhere.

Growls.

Grunts.

*Howls.*

And my Omega… *screaming on the bed.*

# ASHLYN

## NOMAD LANDS, CANADA
## A MINUTE OR SO EARLIER

*THE WARDS HAVE FALLEN. Every last one of them.*

It's a chilling realization that makes the quiet in the house that much more daunting.

I wait, the clock ticking in my mind.

Then a creak sounds from the stairs as the first Alpha ascends.

I don't wait to see his face, just focus on his torso and pull the trigger the moment he appears.

Growls echo from outside and inside the house, my location officially revealed, and boots pound on the hardwood.

I lock and reload, then shoot.

Lock and reload, then shoot.

Again and again.

Until the shotgun is done and all I have left are two revolvers.

I put one in each hand and scream as three Alphas enter the room at once.

I fire in sequence, sending their bodies all over the ground, blood spraying over me and the room.

I can't keep this up for much longer.

There are far more of them than I have bullets. But I just keep *firing*.

Until the *click* tells me I'm out, the sound echoing through my spirit in a wave of agony.

Because the final second has counted down.

*It's done.*

However, I can't just sit and take it, so I come up on my knees with a snarling scream, daring the Alphas to try to take me.

It doesn't matter that my mind is half gone to my heat.

*I. Will. Not. Submit.*

And I demonstrate that with a guttural scream right as Grey materializes in the room, his eyes round as he finds me in the middle of the bed, covered in brain matter and other unmentionable bloody pieces.

Then a growl sounds from the door, and he charges forward to take the Alpha down.

Grey releases a furious rumble that vibrates me to my core and causes me to fall onto the bed, my wolf giving in to her Alpha's call. Only it was a sound of dominance and aggression that he released for all the others around us, followed by a howl that shouts his claim for everyone to hear.

*Mine*, that sound says. *This Omega is* mine.

Which is how I know I've fallen into a dream state.

Because none of this is real.

It can't be happening.

Grey is with his sister now, saving her and taking her to safety.

He can't be here. That's not what the visions have shown in the past.

It's a trick.

*My mind's way of finding peace while my body is destroyed...*

"Ashlyn." Grey's voice rolls over me, the tone so authentic that I smile.

"Alpha." That's all I can say. My insides are on fire, and I'm moments away from losing my grasp on reality. But I want to remember this fantasy—the one where Grey chooses me.

Because no one has ever chosen me before.

I've always sacrificed everything for others, never expecting anything in return.

But it feels nice to dream about being put first for once.

*To be saved...*

I sigh as Grey's scent surrounds me. *Snow falling over evergreens.* It's so strong that I can almost believe he's real.

Just like his purr.

It's a vibration against my ear that pleases my inner wolf.

*The memories of our time together are helping,* I realize. *He'll never know what that meant to me.*

"Ashlyn," he murmurs, his lips against my ear. "Not only am I very real, but I can hear your thoughts."

My lips curl. *Then this most certainly is the best dream I've ever had.*

"Not a dream, little riddler," he says as something wet touches my skin. "Now wake up so I can bathe you."

My eyelashes flutter, the surroundings confusing and not quite right.

Because all I see is white marble and obsidian tiles.

We're in a modern bathroom, sitting in a large shower.

I blink, certain I'm seeing things. *Where are we?*

"My lair in Lunar Sector," he replies, addressing my

thought out loud. "But we're both covered in blood, so unless you want me to knot you like this, I suggest you let me clean us up."

I grab his shoulders and try to focus on him. He just said *knot*. And I very much want that, yes. *Why bother cleaning us up if we're just going to get dirty again?* I wonder.

He lowers his face to mine so our noses are within an inch of one another. "Because I don't fancy fucking my mate when she's covered in another Alpha's blood. Even if it is fucking hot how you shot all those assholes with my guns."

Water splashes down around us, causing me to glance upward at the showerhead.

I wince, not a fan of the sensation. It feels wrong. All I want is to be stroked and licked and *fucked*.

"Soon, mate," Grey says to me, his hands beginning to roam, but not in the way I desire.

He's using soap to clean the crimson stains from my skin.

I have no idea how we got here. How he arrived in time. How he changed fate.

But I... I'm not sad. I'm elated. I'm thrilled, even.

So thrilled that I lean forward and sink my teeth into his pec, just to prove to myself that this is real.

He growls.

I growl back.

Then another layer of our bond seems to settle into place.

A layer I didn't realize was missing.

Because Z-Clan Omegas never have to mark their fated mates.

*But he's not all Z-Clan Alpha,* I realize, my eyes widening. *V-Clan Alphas need that reciprocated bite...*

Grey threads his fingers through my hair and pulls my

head back so he can stare into my eyes. "I'm going to knot you for fucking days, Omega. Make you come so damn hard that you can barely breathe. And then I'm going to bite you again. Because I can. Because I want to. Because I *need* to."

"I might bite you back," I warn him.

"I fucking hope you do," he admits. "Now be a good girl and stand up for me so I can finish washing you off."

My legs move to obey his command, my body seemingly his to control.

Because of my heat.

Or maybe… maybe because it's simply him. Us.

I don't know.

And I don't fight it.

I just revel in the feel of his hands on me, all while trying to hold back my groans from the mounting agony within.

I need a knot. I need relief. *I need to be filled.*

"Here," he says, pulling me back into his lap after rinsing himself off. My thighs part over him, and my insides practically weep as he places his cock right at my entrance. "Take me, mate. Ride me and make me yours."

Oh, I like the sound of that.

I slide right down and groan as he fills me completely. The sensation steals the air from my lungs, causing my head to fall against his shoulder. All I want to do is whimper with relief. But I'm too afraid I might wake up, that I'll experience the horrors of my mind.

Horrors I can't stop thinking about now as tears fall from my eyes.

Grey wraps his arms around me, bathing me in his strength. "You're safe, Ash," he whispers. "I've got you. I'm here. And I will always fucking choose you, little riddler. You're my fated half. My Omega. *My mate.*"

His purr ignites with the words, swathing me in a sea of soothing energy. I lose myself in the comfort for a long moment, simply existing as I try to master my emotions and my mind.

But it's all so raw.

I hear Grey's mind recounting what happened in Kodiak Sector, how his brother—the man I saw in Nikiski's vision—has been manipulating their twin-bond for a century.

Which explains a lot of the haphazard prophecies where my own mating was concerned.

His brother was using Nikiski to manipulate my seeing abilities, forcing me to foresee skewed events.

Everything was hazy for a reason.

And the changes in our paths... they weren't really changes. They were truths.

We were always destined to mate.

But Spruce wouldn't let me *see* that.

He wanted me alone. Scared. Willing to sacrifice everything. All while thinking Grey chose someone else.

It was a cruel manipulation.

One we not only survived but overcame.

*Together*.

Grey palms my cheek, his gaze seeking mine as he pulls me in for a sweet kiss. "This is just the beginning of us, Ash. I don't need fortune-telling abilities to foresee that we're going to do amazing things together."

"Like take down the shadow organization?" I suggest, groggy from fighting off my heat.

"Like take down the shadow organization," he echoes. "With help from others."

I nod. "Nikiski knows things, I think."

"Yes," he agrees. "I believe she does."

His forehead falls to mine.

And we just breathe for a minute.

Then I subtly shift my hips. "Can you foresee what comes next?" I ask him.

He smiles. "Not what, but who. And it's you, of course," he murmurs, his hands reaching up to cup my breasts. "Now ride me, mate. Take us into the future."

"I'm more concerned with the present right now," I reply, squeezing my walls around him. "I'm not going to be lucid much longer."

"Then you'd better start moving, Ash. I want at least two orgasms from you while you're aware." He tugs on my hair, angling my head back. "Then I'll take good care of you while you're in heat."

"Knotting me for days?"

"Knotting you for days," he echoes. "I'm going to take every fucking hole, little riddler, and bathe you in my fucking cum."

I shudder, his words inspiring a fresh wave of slick between my thighs. "Yes, please, Alpha."

"Fuck me, Omega." He adds a slight slap to my rump. "*Fuck me now.*"

I do.

Because I want to.

Because I choose him.

Because we're soulmates.

Bonded.

Meant to be together forever.

And as I fall apart in his lap, I realize there are no more horrific visions of our future.

Only a strengthening bond. Love. *And happiness.*

How interesting that this dance with fate began with me falling into the ice lake. Then continued after being saved from the icy shores of Kodiak Sector. And culminated in a warm shower in Lunar Sector.

The evolution of a relationship. Of fate. *Of us.*

# GREY

## LUNAR SECTOR

ASHLYN'S light hair is a stark contrast to my black linen sheets. But I rather like it. Especially since she's currently crawling all over my bed to turn it into *our* nest.

I lean against the post, watching her work.

She's still in the throes of her heat, my aroused Omega needing my knot every hour.

I don't mind.

Taking care of her is the best fucking feeling in the world.

"I can't wait to meet your wolf," I tell her, longing to see her white fur. I know it'll be the same color as my own.

She glances back at me, her big blue eyes dancing over me and landing appreciatively on my knot. But rather than reach for it, she goes back to her task of moving pillows around and stuffing clothes into specific places. My sheets are all tangled up as well, something she did with her legs.

"Do you need any more blankets?" I ask.

Ashlyn looks at me again.

And then resumes her task.

She's done this a lot these last few days, her nonverbal behavior rather amusing, considering her penchant for riddles.

All she wants is for me to use my mouth in other ways that don't involve talking, which is fine by me. I love the way she tastes. Love making her come. Fuck, I'm pretty sure I love *her*.

Which feels a little insane, but her mind is fucking fascinating. I knew she was altruistic before. However, hearing some of her memories and her thought processes around them drives the point home even more.

This Omega is special and not just because she can see the future.

She's an amazing woman, too. Carefully crafting phrases and words to help others find a destined path.

Sacrificing herself to ensure her friends survive.

Ensuring I found my sister, no matter the personal cost.

She's a martyr.

It's a trait I admire, but one we will be discussing more when she's of sound mind. Because she can't keep putting herself in danger to save others.

My wolf won't allow it.

Instead, we'll work together.

Grow as a mated pair.

Embrace the future as bondmates.

Fortunately, I don't seem to have acquired any new fortune-telling talents from her. But I'm pleased she can make runes. Those will serve her well for protection.

"Alpha." She presents her rump, making me smirk.

"You want to christen the nest?" I ask, coming to kneel behind her and rest my cock against her pretty little ass.

"Knot me."

Her demand is cute. I press a kiss to her shoulder blade, then spin her around and flatten her on her back.

She growls, clearly having wanted me to fuck her from behind.

Too bad for her, I want to do it from the front so I can kiss her talented mouth.

I slide into her in a single thrust, her slick abundant and hot.

She arches into me, and I palm her breast, then lean down to press my lips to hers. She opens for me, waiting for my tongue. Then scratches her nails down my back to coax me into moving.

I love this feral side of her. It matches my beast's savage needs.

And it makes fucking so much more fun.

Because she gives as good as she takes.

She also appears to be quite fond of marking, something she does now by biting my bottom lip.

I return the gesture, and she cries out, then grabs my shoulders and ruts up into me.

She's strong for an Omega. And I fucking love that.

"You're perfect," I praise her. "And your pussy feels fucking amazing around my cock."

She pants against my mouth, begging me without words to give her what she needs.

It doesn't take long, our bodies primed for one another and shattering together in a roar of ecstasy.

Our bliss goes on for hours, her cunt milking my knot until I swear there's nothing left inside me.

Only then does she roll into my arms, her palm finding my purring chest, and says, "I would love to go for a run with you, Alpha Grey."

My lips twitch. "How long have you been lucid?"

"Off and on since I started creating our nest," she admits. "But I rather enjoyed making you knot me."

"*Making* me knot you?" I laugh. "Little riddler, you don't need to *make* me do anything. I've already told you that I want to live inside you."

She smiles. "Maybe for my next heat."

"Are you having a vision?" I ask, mostly teasing. That part of her mind is locked away, hidden from our bond, which is absolutely for the best. I have no interest in fortune-telling.

"If I was, I wouldn't tell you." She taps my nose. "I wouldn't want to risk changing the future."

"Hmm." I go up on my elbow and look at her. "About the future, I took one of those male birth control pills for this cycle. I wasn't sure of your thoughts on kids."

She stares at me. "I like children."

"That's not the same as wanting them."

"I want them," she tells me. "But not yet. We're not ready."

I nod, certain now that she's seen something. "I'll wait for your confirmation."

"You won't need my confirmation; you'll know." Her cryptic words confirm my suspicion about her foreseeing something. "We're going to take down the shadow organization first, make the world safer... for children."

I frown. "You've *seen* us doing that?"

"No." She sounds annoyed by that fact. "So we're just going to have to make it our reality."

"I accept that challenge."

"That part I already know," she says, rolling her eyes. "It's Cael we have to convince."

My brow furrows. "He's been trying to take down that

group for as long as I have. He won't need to be convinced of anything."

"Oh, I'm not talking about that."

I stare at her. "Of course you're not." Because why wouldn't we jump topics in the middle of a conversation?

I nearly huff a laugh.

*Life with a seer.*

"It's related," she murmurs, still cryptic. "Once he accepts, we'll work as a team. But he has to believe, too."

"I have no idea what you're talking about, little riddler."

She smiles. "I know, but you will soon." She snuggles into me. "Thanks for not fighting fate, mate. From what I've seen, rejecting destiny will be exhausting."

I consider her words and know she's still talking about Cael.

*What destiny is he going to reject?* I wonder.

Then still when I remember my sister's whispers about seeing Cael every night.

"Oh, fuck…" My sister thinks Cael is her fated mate. "That can't be right." It's actually the opposite of right. It's fucking *wrong*.

Ashlyn shrugs. "Time will tell." She yawns. "I would like to properly meet her tomorrow, please. I'm still not sure what 'seven' means."

"Seven on a clock from the position where I found you in the water," I explain.

Ashlyn blinks up at me. "Oh." Her lips twist. "I should have figured that out."

"You sent them to find me in Kodiak Sector," I tell her. "That's all they truly needed."

And even then, I had it mostly handled without them.

Well, after Cillian helped, anyway.

I would have to thank him later.

"Lunch with Ivana and Cillian," Ashlyn says, smiling. "Yes."

"I didn't actually say anything, Ash."

"No, but I saw the plan forming and can see the end results. I approve."

I glare at her. "So you can share that tidbit about the future but can't tell me what's going to happen between my sister and my best friend?"

She shrugs. "Their future is too important for me to meddle in or potentially change. Lunch with Ivana and Cillian is far more harmless."

"I see," I murmur, still narrowing my gaze at her. "How about telling me when I'll knot you again?"

"Oh, right now, of course," she replies, her hand wrapping around my base. "But you're going to come in my mouth first because I'm hungry."

And I'm instantly hard. "Then you'd better straddle my face and feed me too, mate."

Her eyes glitter. "Dessert for two, coming right up."

But she kisses me instead of moving into position, her tongue lazy against mine.

"Can I change my introduction?"

I frown. "Your introduction?"

She nods. "I want to reintroduce myself."

"To my cock?" I ask hopefully.

"No, Alpha." She swats playfully at my chest. "To you."

I arch a brow, admittedly intrigued. "All right."

She smiles and sits up, causing her breasts to sway— which is really fucking distracting.

"Hi. I'm Ashlyn, Z-Clan Omega. I didn't join the mating program to find a mate, but I found one anyway. And I'm really not upset about it."

"No?"

She shakes her head. "No. Not at all. He has a massive knot and a wicked tongue. Oh, and he's a beast in the nest."

I chuckle. "Well, it's nice to meet you, Ashlyn. I'm Grey, a hybrid Alpha who is really fucking hard and wants to knot his Omega now."

"You should probably do that, then," she tells me. "Maybe claim her again, too."

"I'm starting to think you have a biting fetish, mate."

"Only with you," she murmurs. "Now put your hands behind your head. I'm going to suffocate you with my slick."

"*Fuck*, Ash." The things this female has started saying to me…

"Yes, after dessert," she murmurs, leaning in to kiss me as I move my arms to where she requested.

"You realize I'm indulging your propensity for topping from the bottom, yes?"

Her lips curl, her eyes glimmering with amusement. "Don't worry, Alpha. I'll submit when you demand it."

With that, she moves and gives me her pussy to lick.

Which I do.

*Thoroughly.*

Just as she takes me deep in her mouth, her tongue swirling around my head while she palms my cock.

It's exhilarating and arousing and so fucking phenomenal that I nearly drown her with my seed.

But she swallows it all.

Because she's my perfect mate.

My beautiful Omega.

*My Ashlyn.*

"I want to go for that run now," she whispers, her voice a little hoarse from our "dessert" activities. "Can you shadow us somewhere to shift?"

I almost recommend a shower first. Or food. But I can hear the eagerness in her mind, so I wrap her in my arms and take us to one of my favorite places in Lunar Sector.

It's a flat patch of land covered in snow. But it's quiet and peaceful and perfect for our wolves to finally meet.

"Thank you," Ashlyn says, and I understand that she's thanking me for more than just this experience. She's thanking me for changing her future. For opening her eyes to a new destiny. *For choosing her...*

"I thank fate for pairing us," I tell her, meaning it. "Now let's introduce our beasts."

I decide to shift first and love the way her mouth gapes open after I shake out my coat.

My wolf is huge.

And she obviously *likes* that he's huge.

"You're beautiful," she tells me, her hand reaching for my wolf's coat. He leans into her, purring in response to her touch.

Then she takes a step back and reveals her petite white wolf.

*You're wrong, little riddler,* I think at her. You *are the beautiful one.*

Her wolf preens in response, then does a little bound into the snow.

I'm not sure when she last shifted, but I'm guessing it's been a while.

Because her animal seems elated to be free.

My beast understands the feeling and purrs even louder. Then he nips at her heel, demanding a game of chase.

*I suppose some games are worth playing,* I muse.

Especially ones that involve chasing my mate.

The moment she takes off, my wolf excitedly starts

after her, and we engage in our first official dance as bonded wolves.

Frolicking in the snow.

Chasing one another.

And embracing our destiny.

*As eternal mates.*

# EPILOGUE

## CAEL

"They're already mated," I tell Kieran O'Callaghan. "What would you have me do?"

"Alpha Grey should have followed proper protocols," the Blood Sector King replies, his displeasure clear. "They were both part of the program."

"Yes, and while I respect the purpose of the mating program, Ashlyn and Grey were never meant to be candidates. And we both know that Ashlyn also didn't join to find a mate."

"Intention doesn't automatically remove an Omega from the candidate list."

"But choice should," I counter, making the Alpha's jaw clench visibly on the screen. "She *chose* Grey, Kieran." I forgo the title formalities, something I rarely do. But the Blood Sector King has started to feel more like an ally lately than an adversary.

I like that he cares about Omegas.

It's a trait we share.

"I realize this may put you in an awkward place in

terms of explanations, but nothing untoward happened," I stress.

He snorts. "And how long did Alpha Grey have Ashlyn in his care before finally returning to V-Clan territory?"

I smile. "Perhaps you should ask Ashlyn that question?"

His dark eyes hold mine, the intensity causing my wolf to stir inside me. "As it is, she's already sent me a note via a secure channel she shouldn't have access to."

"I would feign surprise, but I'm tired," I admit. It's not a lie. I'm fucking exhausted.

I've spent the last few days avoiding a certain Omega.

Nikiski.

My best friend's little sister.

The poor girl seems to have a hero-worship complex, thinking that because I saved her life, we're destined to be mates.

And my inner wolf is far too intrigued by the prospect of what kind of *hero worship* she might be into.

It's so fucking wrong.

What's even more wrong is the fact that her naked body and all those damn curves will not leave my mind.

We fucking saved her from being held hostage in a cave. And my knot is over here wanting to give her a different kind of recovery therapy.

"Then I suppose we can discuss your call with Oros another day," Kieran says, yanking my focus back to him with a sharp tug.

"Oros?" I repeat, feigning confusion. "What call with Oros?"

Kieran considers me for a moment. "You know, Dixon and Lorcan would make a good team. Perhaps we can let them play together someday… online."

The call goes dead with that not-so-cryptic statement, and I sigh.

Dixon has notoriously been my means of gathering data on others, his technology skills superior. He's very aware that Lorcan, the newly proclaimed Night Sector Prince, is equally skilled. Or perhaps even more skilled.

Because it seems he somehow learned of my call with Gold Sector.

A call I need to follow up on to schedule a time to meet in person.

*Another day*, I decide, lounging in my office chair. Another day that will undoubtedly be very soon, though.

*Obsidian Sector.*

I've been gathering research on that Drakon-Clan domain since our call. But there isn't much information available.

And there hasn't been a lot of time to thoroughly investigate Kodiak Sector since our raid last week either.

But it's all linked somewhat.

The estrus parties.

The Omega slave trade.

Whatever the fuck Obsidian Sector is doing in those Omega labs.

I tap my pen against the desk.

For the first time in a very long time, I feel like we're close to uncovering the truth.

Once we do, we can take it all down.

Dismantle the horrific activities for good.

At least until the next asshole makes a power grab and decides to re-create it all over again.

I palm the back of my neck and growl, irritated with the fate of the world. Irritated with Alpha kind. And irritated with my wolf's newfound obsession with fucking strawberries.

That's what Nikiski smells like.

The scent is everywhere.

Taunting my inner beast.

Making me think of her naked body pressed against mine for safety.

How my purr roared to life.

How she fit into my side.

How she boldly looked at me and said, "Take me home, Alpha. I'm ready to be yours."

The female was in fucking captivity yet seems to be perfectly fine. It's an act, I'm sure. But it showcases how damn strong she is, which is an aphrodisiac to my beast.

I just want to go toe-to-toe with her and push all her buttons.

Which is ridiculous. And never going to fucking happen.

She's an Omega under my care in Lunar Sector now. I would send her to the Sanctuary in Night Sector, but Grey will likely want to keep her close.

So she's under my jurisdiction now.

And very much off-limits.

*Fated mates*, I think with a grunt. *There is no such thing as fated mates for an Alpha like me.*

Pushing the foolishness away, I focus on wrapping things up in my office. Then I close everything down.

It's time for a run in wolf form.

I have anxious energy to expel.

*And an Omega to forget…*

**Cael's story is next in *Lunar Sector*…**

**Curious about what's happening in the Drakon-Clan world?** Check out *Gold Sector* (Oros & Taliana)

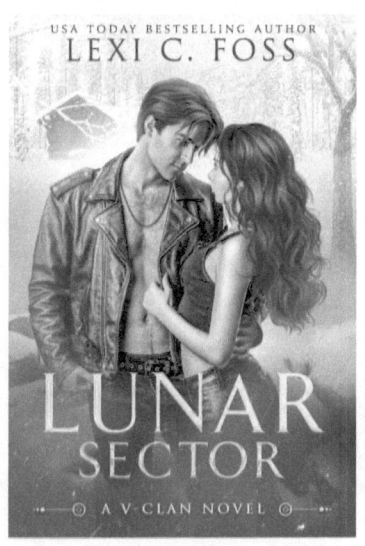

## Lunar Sector

**My fated mate doesn't believe in destiny.
When I tell him he's mine, he rejects our bond.
But I'm not giving up…**

Prince Cael has haunted my dreams for a century.
A perk and a consequence of my psychic talents.

When I finally see him in person, I tell him how I feel.
Only for him to inform me that V-Clan Alphas don't have
fated mates.

Well, that's too bad because Z-Clan Omegas do.
And this Alpha is *mine*.

Our fate is intertwined with the shadow organization he's
been hunting for the last century.

He has no idea what's coming. But I've dreamt of our future.
It's dark. Twisted. And riddled with death.

If he doesn't accept our bond, it could change everything. I'm going to do whatever it takes to make him stop seeing me as his best friend's little sister and start embracing me as his *mate*.

**Author's Note:** *Lunar Sector* is a standalone shifter romance featuring a dark world with knotting, nesting, growling, and a whole hell of a lot of purring. Prince Cael might be in denial about his fated mate, but when he falls, he'll fall hard…

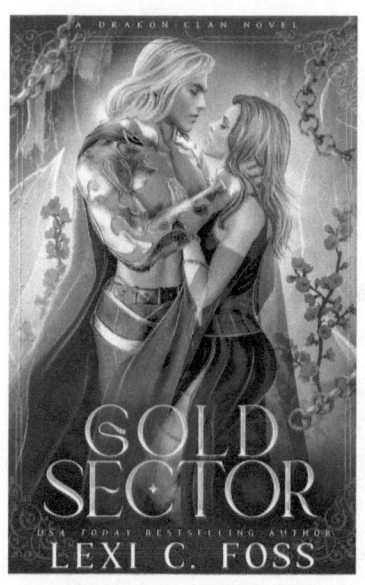

## Gold Sector

I'm a broken Omega.
A hybrid wolf shifter
An abomination to dragonkind.
If these Alpha dragons find out, they're going to send me
back to the nomad lands... *to die*.

They already suspect that I'm something "other."
Hence the evaluations and trials laid out before me.

So when my Alpha guard offers me a set of magical gold
coins, I try to use them to buy favor with the Royal Court.
Except they want *more*.

To survive, I strike a deal with my handsome guard—I'll
give him whatever he wants in exchange for more of his
golden enchantments.

There's just one problem.
I underestimated the cost of this agreement.
Because it turns out there's only one thing my Alpha guard wants.
And it's the one thing I can't give…
*An heir.*

**Author's Note:** *Gold Sector* is a "Rumpelstiltskin" retelling that features a fast-paced, fast-burn plot and a happily-ever-after ending.

USA Today Bestselling Author Lexi C. Foss loves to play in dark worlds, especially the ones that bite. She lives in North Carolina with her family. When not writing, she's busy crossing items off her travel bucket list, or chasing eclipses around the globe. She's quirky, consumes way too much coffee, and loves to swim.

Want access to the most up-to-date information for all of Lexi's books? Sign-up for her newsletter here.

Lexi also likes to hang out with readers on Facebook in her exclusive readers group - Join Here.

*Where To Find Lexi:*
www.LexiCFoss.com

www.ingramcontent.com/pod-product-compliance
Lightning Source LLC
Chambersburg PA
CBHW020318260626
47156CB00004B/1277